20 TURNS OF A

KALEIDOSCOPE

a series of short stories

Jonathan Whiterod

reluctant stories

hide within my shadow, while

yearning for the light

Haiku by Jonathan Whiterod

Dedicated to Kevin, for giving me both the courage and the audacity to publish this book.

Table of Contents

1 Baby Brady 4
2 The Dark Place 22
3 Adam & E-5 40
4 Annie Walker 67
5 Shooter In The Park 71
6 The Bad Lamp 79
7 Ever Decreasing Circles 99
8 The Velvet Shroud 120
9 Letting Go 128
10 Out Of This World 134
11 Amber, Jade & Ruby 149
12 Annooska 156
13 Creep Feeling 169
14 Barry & Barbra 175
15 While The Kettle Boiled - Miss z 186
16 While The Kettle Boiled - High Voltage! 191
17 While The Kettle Boiled - Alison Walker 196
18 A Christmas Miracle 204
19 I Love You, I'm Sorry, I Love You 216
20 Heterochromia Iridium 224

1 Baby Brady

Jesse drove his car over the level crossing and made a right turn onto the dual carriageway. Apple maps had marked the whole route as amber, adding to his already bad mood. He reached into the door bin for some sweets, but the bag was full of empty wrappers. A seagull shit on his windscreen, splatting loudly and making him jump. As he turned on the wipers, the large blob of off-white excrement smeared across the screen. Pulling the lever towards him, Jesse remembered that he hadn't filled the washer bottle. Fucking. Hell.

Peering through the milky windscreen, Jesse navigated the traffic back to his home. It had been a long day. Baby Brady had kept him awake most of the previous night, which was fucking typical. He'd had a huge presentation to make at work that day and doing it on about two hours of fractured sleep had been awesome. He'd gotten ready for work in such a sleep deprived stupor that he'd failed to notice the snot all over his Hugo Boss jacket. It was pointed out to him just as he was about to start the presentation by Andy, a work colleague who never missed an opportunity to undermine him. Removing his jacket, Jesse was horrified to find huge sweat marks under his arms. The strong, black coffee he'd been drinking all morning in search of that illusive caffeine buzz, kicked in all at once. His head spun as he became twitchy and agitated, his bowels objecting to the caffeine offensive and threatening to empty themselves at any moment. Jesse blustered and hurried his way through the presentation, often losing his train of thought and finding it more difficult to pick it back up again each time. He hopped gently from foot to foot in an effort to stave off imminent, uncontrollable defecation as the presentation finally came to an end. When he stopped talking, the room fell completely silent, the only sound being the cool, whooshing air emitted by the a/c unit. The clients looked bemused and turned to Jenny, his boss, for confirmation. She didn't acknowledge them. Instead, her cold, expressionless face was fixed on Jesse, the only thing giving her away being a snarling curl in the corner of her mouth. Meanwhile, a sickening grin spread slowly across Andy's smug face as he turned to Jenny, and whispered poison into her ear.

Later that afternoon Jesse was sitting in his soulless cubicle, staring blankly at the computer monitor and considering whether he could sleep with his eyes open. An unidentified sound distracted him, and as he lazily searched for its source, his tired eyes rested on the photo he'd pinned to the cubicle wall of himself and Baby Brady at the Christmas Wonderland a couple of months before. There was a brightness in his eyes that he hadn't seen in some time. A lightness to his expression and features. Lately it had been replaced by an almost permanently furrowed brow, dark half-moons under each eye and the feeling of a weight pressing down on the top of his head.

Jesse looked at Brady's beaming face protruding from under his reindeer onesie. He'd had a streaming cold at the time and his resulting red nose finished the look off perfectly. Both faces beamed back at him, almost mockingly now. He was so unhappy.

This isn't how the agency had sold it to him. It was supposed to enrich his life, help him to feel complete. Sure, the first few weeks were good. His firm had granted him some paternity leave which had enabled him to get everything set up, read the books and do the classes. With no outside distractions, Jesse had enjoyed this new focus. Less on himself and more on this little bundle of life with his wispy blond hair, sky blue eyes and chubby little limbs. It was refreshing, invigorating even. Jesse had spent a small fortune on designer outfits, accessories and gadgets and loved nothing more than dressing up Baby Brady and showing him off to his friends. His Insta blew up every time that he posted. And Baby Brady seemed to love all of the attention, as he cooed his way through the day, eating his mushy food without fuss. He'd sleep through the night, and hardly ever cry. They were quite the envy of Jesse's friends, and foolishly, he took the credit for it. He had thought that he was knocking this parenthood thing out of the park, but boy did it change when he returned to work. He had employed the services of a nanny, Max. On the morning that Jesse prepared to return to work and leave them together for the first time, Baby Brady hadn't seemed unsettled at all. Jesse kissed him goodbye and left Max his numbers in case of emergencies. He was just pulling up into the staff car park when he got the first call. There were two more by lunch time and he had to leave work early that afternoon to relieve Max. It seemed that Baby Brady did not like Max. He'd screamed almost as soon as Jesse had left and only stopped screaming to catch his breath. Which he very rarely needed to do, it seemed. He wouldn't eat, he wouldn't drink. He wouldn't sleep either, but he would bite and scratch and kick out at Max like a wild animal. But when Jesse arrived home, it was as if a switch had been flicked. Baby Brady instantly calmed at seeing Jesse's face. The tears subsided, the lashing out relented, and he realised that he was both hungry, and thirsty. From the moment Jesse walked in the door, Baby Brady was stuck on him like glue.

To his credit, Max was a professional. He had a firm but kind nature and took all of Baby Brady's performances in his stride. After he'd gotten over that first traumatic day, Max regrouped and buckled down, tirelessly working with Baby Brady to gain his trust and love. And it worked. Too well. Over a period of weeks, the object of Baby Brady's love started to shift. Jesse was working long hours, often he would leave at 7am and not return until Baby Brady was already in bed. Slowly, the problem started to reverse. Baby Brady would visibly stiffen one seeing Jesse return home and would cry, scream, kick and bite his way through the evening until he tired himself out and fell asleep. But he only needed an hour or so to recharge before being ready to go again.

Jesse was exhausted. And resentful. Any bond that he'd established in those early weeks was all but gone. Work had initially been supportive of his life choice but were now of the opinion that they had fulfilled that duty once he had returned from paternity leave. And his friends, who were initially supportive and accepting, became distant and unavailable. He couldn't shake the feeling that as much as they had gushed about how brave he was, about how wonderful it was that we lived in a time where this was possible, that they secretly saw him as a bit of a joke and didn't take him or his situation as a new parent seriously. They never offered to have Baby Brady over for play dates. When Jesse invited them over and made it difficult for them to refuse, they didn't abandon their children to play together like they did with their other friends. Instead, they stayed close, with one eye on their baby and the other on Baby Brady.

Jesse was pulled back to reality by the harsh trill of his phone.

"Jesse, have you got a minute?" Click, the line went dead.

Jesse took a deep breath and hauled himself into Jenny's office.

"Don't sit down Jesse, this won't take long. Today was a shambles. You *looked* like shit. You looked like you *needed* a shit. And you *talked* a load of shit. It was all *shit*. Go home and get your *shit* together". Visibly irritated, she got up from her desk and started to pace the office. "You've been with the company for a long time Jesse, and you've deposited a certain amount of goodwill in the bank. But you've blown through it. We were all behind this whole baby thing, but it's impacting your work. Which impacts me. I don't get it, but whatever. It all seems a bit unnatural, but I respect your life choices. But like I said to Brenda when she began identifying as Brendan; leave your cock at the door. Well, that doesn't translate exactly to your situation, but you get where I'm going. And where *you're* going is home. To sort out said *shit*. By the end of the week. Or I'll sort it out for you".

Jesse winced a little, his face burning with shame. He was about to stammer a reply when he realised that this wasn't a conversation. She was already on the phone, berating a client. Looking up from her monitor and surprised to see him still there, her eyes went wide, and she held up her free hand as if to say, 'what the fuck?'

Pulling up onto the drive, Jesse switched off the engine and took a second. He was overwhelmed with nausea at the thought of what was waiting for him inside. He began to feel that he had made a mistake. He wasn't cut out for this, what was he thinking? He was angry at the agency for making it sound so easy, for convincing him that he could have it all. He felt duped. He was a salesman himself; he should have seen through the pitch. He was lost in swirling thoughts of doubt and resentment when Max tapped on the car window.

"Jesus, Max. What the fuck?"

"Sorry Jesse, but you're late and I have a date to get to. Zach? With the hair and the cabin by the lake?"

Jesse did remember and was quietly jealous. Jealous of Max having a life and being able to go on dates, and jealous of Zach.

"I know, I'm sorry Max, I really am. I was just finishing off a work call", he lied. "I'm coming in now".

Walking through the front door, Jesse was greeted by what had become the signature scent of his home. A heady of mix of vomit, shit, sour milk and wet wipes. It was a powerful aroma, one which not even the expensive smart home-fragrance system could cut its way through.

"So, Brady is all ready for bed. He's just had his milk, so all you really need to do is to put him down".

Max was still holding Brady and both he and Jesse were doing a strange dance around the handover as they knew what was about to happen. Max tentatively extended out his arms, holding a currently quiet and passive Baby Brady. Jesse gingerly held out his arms to take him. But as soon as Baby Brady entered Jesse's airspace, the wailing, screaming, crying, kicking and clawing begun. Over the din, Max mouthed 'see you tomorrow morning – have a good evening'. He hadn't meant it to be sarcastic.

As Max pulled off the drive, Jesse felt profoundly alone. He turned Baby Brady around to look at his face which was bright red, and angry. As tears sprung from squeezed shut eyes in almost cartoon-like fashion, his tiny body flexed and convulsed as if he were allergic to Jesse's very touch. Overwhelmed, Jesse started to walk slowly around the room, rocking Baby Brady back and forth in an effort to pacify him. "I love you Baby Brady, I love you so much. Why don't you love me?", he repeated over and over, and when Baby Brady's apparent fury refused to acquiesce, Jesse's sense of desperation became almost too much to take. The gentle rocking became less gentle, instead turning into a manic swing from side to side as Jesse's hushed, cajoling tones gave way to a desperate scream. "I LOVE YOU BABY BRADY – WHY DON'T YOU LOVE ME BACK!" he yelled at the top of his voice. He was suddenly aware that he was no longer rocking Baby Brady, he was shaking him. He stopped. Baby Brady wasn't crying, flailing or kicking. Instead, he stared passively with unreadable eyes into Jesse's panicked, horror-stricken face. For a terrible, gut-wrenching moment Jesse thought that he had broken him in some way. There was a heart-stopping silence that seemed to last forever. And then as if a switch had been flipped or a circuit reconnected, Baby Brady quickly resumed his wailing, flailing and screaming, now with added resolve. Sickened at what had just happened, at what had *nearly* just happened, Jesse marched across the lounge and placed Baby Brady into the play pen. He no longer trusted himself.

In the kitchen, Jesse poured a large glass of red and downed it like water on a hot day. I can't do this, he thought. I can't do this anymore. Jesse was lost in this dark place when his phone rang. Checking the caller ID, he saw that it was Jenny. If it had been anyone else, he'd have let it go to answer phone. But many a career had ended by letting Jenny go to answer phone. He took a breath and tried to muster some of his old self.

"Jenny, hi. What can I d…"

"Jesse, I won't beat around the preverbal. I'm giving the Masterson account to Andy. You really blew it today and they are talking about moving their business. I can't allow that to happen. Andy has been great and is happy to add this to his current case load. He's a real team player that one. Someone you can count on, you know?" She paused and Jesse didn't know whether that was a cue or whether she was just talking a breath.

"Jenny, listen. Today was a one off. You know me, I would usually have run rings around those guys, charming the two-million-euro account right out of their hands. It's this thing with Brady. It just threw me for a loop today but I'm sorting things. I am. Honestly Jenny, trust me, I just need a few days to get things levelled out". Jesse hated the pleading tone of his voice, and he knew that Jenny would hate it even more.

"We just don't have a few fucking days for you to get your bougie child-care issues sorted. Masterson are coming back in tomorrow for a do-over of that presentation. Andy spent two hours on the phone and practically sold his soul to get them back. Its tomorrow or we lose it. *You* lose it".

That fucking Andy. That fucking cock sucking Andy, Jesse seethed. He was so far up Jenny's arse, it was indecent. Everyone could see it. Everyone knew it.

But for whatever reason, Jenny was blind to it. Jesse was thinking fast. And panicking.

"Jenny, I will be in the office at 6 am tomorrow morning and I will prepare the shit out of that presentation. I'll pull out every stop and dazzle them with everything I've got. I'll even suck that account managers cock if it helps. You know how he's always rubbing himself under the desk when I'm in the room. I'd do it Jenny, I would. Just give me a chance. I can do this." There was silence at the end of the phone. Just a little creak as Jenny adjusted her grip of the handset. And then a long exhalation.

"Listen, Jesse, I don't want to tell you what to do. You're free to live your life however you choose. And I genuinely don't care what you do outside of work. But you bring it to the office and I then I start caring. If you ask me, you clearly aren't cut out for this parenthood thing. It's just a fad. An accessory. A look for you to try on. You're failing at it Jesse, and you're failing here too. I was just calling today to pass some of your work on to Andy while you got it together. But the more I hear you talk, the less I believe that you can. If you aren't in the office by six tomorrow and if you don't land that account by any means necessary, you can clear out your desk. We can't carry you. We *won't* carry you. Good night, Jesse". Click.

Jesse felt like he'd been punched in the gut. It was so brutal. *She* was so brutal. What a mother fucking bitch. The woman had no soul. She was a machine, a cold, hard, emotionless machine. But machines were rarely wrong. And he *was* failing. His whole world was about to fall out of his arse. And then a darkness came over him, causing his heart to race, and his skin to creep. It made him sick to his stomach, but there was no other way. He'd be judged for it. People would talk. He'd lose friends. But he'd still have his career, his professional reputation. And if anyone doubted his balls at work before, they certainly wouldn't after this. Maybe they would respect him more for it, even fear him a little.

Jesse calmly set his glass down and tightly gripped the edge of the breakfast bar in an effort to steady himself. His hands turned white and started to shake with the effort as Baby Brady ramped up his shrieking to new levels. In an act of sudden decisiveness, he pulled open the kitchen drawer and searched for what he needed. Catching the side of his palm on a serrated knife, he cursed to himself and continued the search, adrenalin numbing the pain. Slamming the drawer shut in frustration, he noticed that he was bleeding. Thinking that he should get a plaster, it came to him. First aid box – that was where he had hidden it. He practically ran to the walk-in store cupboard and pulled down the red tin box. Sorting through the plasters, tubes of cream and drugs, he found what he'd been looking for. He grabbed it and flew across the kitchen and punched through the swing door, into the lounge. Coming from the muted protection of the kitchen, the intensity of the crying was overwhelming. Baby Brady was purple with rage. Jesse slowed as he warily approached the play pen. The Noah's Ark mobile chimed surreally through the awful din. He'd loved him once. Or at least loved the idea of him. His grip tightened on the tool as Baby Brady looked up at him, his cheeks red raw with tears. As he cried and cried, Jesse realised that he had completely failed him. He'd treated him like an object from the beginning. A new toy. And when things had become difficult, had become real, he'd lost interest. If he started over again now, with the benefit of hindsight, it would end the same way. It was who he was. He just didn't have it in him to give himself over to someone else. He was too selfish, he understood that about himself now. He adjusted his grip on the tool and primed it.

"I'm sorry, I really am. This is for you as much as it is for me. I can't give you what you need. I'm so sorry, I'm so..." Jesse broke down into wild sobs. Through blurry, teared eyes Jesse extended the tool with a trembling hand, holding it to Brady's skin just below his jaw until he felt the gentle tug of a magnetic connection. "I'm sorry", he sobbed as he held the tool in place and pressed the red button. A soft white light pulsed in Baby Brady's left temple, and all at once he became terribly silent, and still. An eerily disembodied voice from somewhere deep inside his tiny chest coldly announced, 'unit deactivated.' Blood dripped from the cut on Jesse's hand, falling onto Baby Brady's dinosaur onesie.

2 The Dark Place

Oh, I'm back. I'll never get used to this. One minute nothing, oblivion. And then I'm here. Wherever 'here' is. I mean that most literally because I have no idea where I am or where I came from, before I was here. I know I'm dead, I know that much. And I remember dying. Cancer. I remember being laid out in the hospice bed, wired up to machines with people hovering nervously around me. Waiting. As was I. It had been a hard slog, and I was done. I gave it my best shot, but you have to know when you're beat. I had the proverbial towel in my hand, and I was ready to throw it in. But there was someone I was waiting to see first. My brother. I knew they'd called him. I heard mum go to the corner of the room and whisper into the phone, her back to me, hunched. I could see her shoulders jumping up and down as she tried to stifle her sobs. "Barry, I think it's time........not long now......you'd better hurry". So, I was waiting. It would kill him (an unfortunate choice of words) to miss seeing me before I went. He is the sensitive one out of the two of us. Always has been. We are twins and identical in appearance, but night and day when it comes to personality. Barry has always been kind to my selfish. Thoughtful to my insensitive. A thinker to my doer.

I'm just five minutes older than him, but those minutes seemed to have set the whole dynamic for our relationship. I was always the older brother as far as he was concerned, the protector. Someone he looked up to. And someone who should look out for him. He needed that from me. But that's just not who I am. I'm reckless and impulsive. And no matter how many times I fall short of his expectations, he always forgives me and keeps coming back. So I was holding on for him, because I knew he needed me to. But I was so tired. I'd been holding on for what felt like an eternity. I'd been holding on ever since I got my diagnosis three years before. I'd just rest a little, I remember thinking, close my eyes until he arrived. But he never did. Well, he did, but not in time.

Looking for the swirling mists in the darkness, I stretch limbs that aren't there. Rub eyes that aren't there. I yawn an impossible yawn; I've no mouth to yawn with and no air to suck in and exhale. It's a very strange feeling to be here, but not really anywhere. It's like a very dark, sightless dream. I'm aware of being somewhere, of existing, but no sense of physical presence. The idea of it, the memory of it – yes. But not the reality of it. I'm aware of being upright, but there is nothing firm beneath me. I can't tell if I'm in a small room or a space a thousand lightyears across. There is a darkness I haven't experienced before. A total absence of anything. No sound, no smell, no touch, no air. It's almost impossible to describe everything that isn't here. The first time it happened I panicked like I'd never known panic before. I gasped for breath, unable to take in any air, clutching at a non-existent throat. It was a while before I realised that I wasn't breathing, but I wasn't suffocating either. I was thrashing around wildly, trying to cling to something. I was completely disorientated. I felt like I was falling, continually in a void of darkness and silence. But I didn't ever crash to the ground, I was just suspended.

Nothing suspended in more nothing. I could go on forever - I might actually have forever – and I still don't think I could make you understand how this feels. So I'll stop trying. Suffice to say, its fucking unsettling.

I'm waiting now. I've been called here, so that is the first stage. I just have to wait. Either the mists will come, and this will develop into something, or it will be a fleeting visit and I'll drop into oblivion again. It's not like I have anything better to do.

***

Barry pulled up his jacket collar and hunched his shoulders against the morning rain as he crossed the street to the jewellers. Autumn leaves gathered in the gutters in beautifully coloured clumps. The sound of rain pouring into the drains filled him with a sense of comfort and warmth. He loved autumn. The way it made him want to retreat indoors, nest under blankets, eat warming foods and make Christmas preparations. The thought caught him off-guard a little and stung. Shaking it off, he pushed open the door and was greeted by the sound of a thousand ticking clocks and a wall of hot, stuffy air that smelled as old as time itself.

He handed his chit to a wiry old woman with pins in her hair and she fussed around in drawers under the counter. He explained that he'd received a text to say that it was ready for collection. After a concerning amount of time, she held aloft his order with what seemed like a little surprise.

"It's here!" she declared gleefully, suggesting that there was a possibility it might not have been.
"Great!" he answered, mirroring her sense of surprise.

Pulling up his collar again, he headed back out into the rain. Taking in a deep breath of damp air, he headed to his usual coffee place. Hands stuffed in pockets, he found the small brown package. He ran his fingers over it tentatively, pressing slightly to feel the shape of what was inside. A lump formed in his throat as his mind began to wander, tears threatening his eyes. Fighting them back, he pushed through the door of the coffee shop.

***

    Ok, I can see the mist coming. Looks like I'm here for a bit longer. When I say mist, I don't so much mean the physical presence of mist, the physical presence of something. It's more the absence of nothing. Which forms something. A misty weakness in the dark void that doesn't give light exactly, just a bit less darkness. It's also the first sign that things are about to get interesting. I can hear some sounds too. That often happens. I can't locate them; they don't seem to come from any direction. They just hang in the air. Coming and going. Fading in and out. Today it's the familiar clatter of cups and saucers. The hissing of steam. Screeching babies and protesting parents. Music that you don't recognise but at the same time sounds familiar, playing just on your threshold of hearing. I'm often drawn here. This is where we used to meet to catch up at the weekend, so it makes sense. Barry is sentimental to a fault.

Wait, what's that? Something familiar, but something I haven't experienced since arriving in the dark place. It's evoking memories. Whoa, it's a smell! I can smell something! That's never happened before. I can fucking smell fucking coffee! And warm pastries. And, gross, baby puke. I focus on the coffee. It's never smelled so good. Nothing ever has. My mind races. What does this mean? It's different this time. I can feel it. I feel exhilarated. I....

***

Barry was playing with the package in his pocket again while waiting for his pumpkin spice latte. He fingered the opening, pushing his finger under the flap of paper and feeling the cool, smooth ring inside. A sudden jolt of electricity surged through him. A pulse of feelings, sensations and memories associated with his brother. Wait, what the.....

"Oh my God, oh my God, oh my GOD! I'm so sorry. Let me get that for you"

The mortified father whipped out an industrial sized pack of wet wipes from under an expensive looking buggy and got to work cleaning up the baby puke from Barry's Nikes.

"Don't worry it's fine, honestly. It's not your fault". Barry's tone of voice was at complete odds with his words.

The dad looked up, hands full of wet wipes dripping with vomit.

"Honestly, it's been a day", he said, "believe it or not, if I had to rate the shitty things that have happened to me today, this wouldn't make the top three"

The poor guy looked like he was about to cry. As he continued to wipe, scrub and dab at Barry's Nikes, Barry noticed that people were beginning to stare.

"Please, stand up. You don't have to do that. I'll just wash them when I get home". Note to self, thought Barry; I'll burn them when I get home.

The overwhelmed father looked at Barry with wide, slightly wild eyes. This guy really has had a day, Barry thought. He took pity on him and paid for his coffee. He'd protested, but Barry insisted. The guy thanked him profusely with the kind of gratitude you reserve for someone who just cured your cancer. And then goes on to solve world hunger. Uncomfortable with the attention he was drawing, Barry assured his new biggest fan that he was most welcome and that he hoped his day got better.

Sitting now in his usual chair, at his usual table, he regarded the empty chair opposite him. The huge void created by its emptiness bellied the physical dimensions of the chair itself. It represented his loss, and it was immense. Too big to be contained by just a chair. By this coffee shop. By this town even. Barry wondered if it could be contained at all. He stared at it, wishing with all his being that Phil could sit there again and mock him from across the table. Rib him about his wokeness. Tell him stories of his latest conquests. And pry too much into his own. But he knew that it was never going to happen. He was gone. Everything that he ever knew about his brother, everything they'd experienced together is, and always would be, confined to past tense. It stung. It was obvious, hardly a great revelation, but the dawning of this was profoundly sad to Barry. He was devastated to have lost Phil. The brother he'd admired and looked up to, who'd seemed able to do anything. Who'd seemed indestructible. To see him slowly wither away into nothing had been almost too much for him to bear. He didn't even get to be there with him at the end, and that's what Barry struggled with the most. He didn't have closure. He just couldn't move on. It all felt so unfinished. If he could just....

He pulled out the package from his pocket and stared at the simple gold band. He didn't know how he felt about it, what he was going to do with it. Wear it? Put it in a drawer for safe keeping? What did it represent? Was it healthy to hang on to it, or would it be a constant reminder, pulling him back to his grief when he was trying to move past it? It had been their grandfathers, left to Phil as the oldest. Phil had worshipped their grandfather and was devastated when he'd died. He would never talk about it. But he never took that ring off. On impulse, Barry put it on his finger.

***

Barry! Hey, Barry! I can see you! Not just the usual hazy, fuzzy outline of you. I can see you as if I'm sat across the table from you in my usual chair! This is epic, this is fucking epic. Barry! It's me, Phil! Can you hear me? Can you see me? Can you sense me? I wish I knew how to reach you. How to tell you it's ok. I'm ok. You're going to be ok. Barry, it's me! I'm here!

My mind is racing at the speed of light, and I feel completely amped. This has never happened before. It's always just been a glimpse here, a glimpse there. I can sometimes hear him. Sometimes make out the outline of him. And then he's gone. As soon as he becomes distracted, as soon as he stops thinking about me, I just vanish back to wherever it is I came from. The dark place. But this is my chance. It feels different. I can connect with him, I know it. I've tried before, by manipulating objects around him to show him that I'm here. But I'm pretty shit at it. Like Patrick Swayze trying to swipe that fucking can on the underground in Ghost. I managed to muster a shadow once. I projected it onto the ceiling one night just after I died when he was crying himself to sleep. I tried to make it look like the Nike trademark tick. Stupid, I know. Stupid. But Nike shopping was kind of our thing. Obviously, he didn't see the shadowy outline of a stretched and distorted Nike tick and realise its profound meaning as a message from his dead older twin brother. Nor did he pick up on the rainbows that I keep producing for him by making light reflect through his kitchen window onto my football shirt which he'd rather creepily hung on his kitchen wall. I told you, he's the sensitive one.

And robins! I've sent him so many fucking robins. They're the only animate object that I've been able to exert any influence over. And I say exert, but they seem to do it willingly. Mostly. I sent one to sit on his bedroom window ledge and sing the same song, at the same time, every morning for a week. The robin got bored in the end. And then there was – oh. I still feel bad about this. It wasn't really my fault, but still. There was this very young robin. A cute little guy, just out of the nest. I was able to persuade him to sit on Barry's doorstep, and continually peck at the door. When Barry eventually relented and got up to see what the noise was, there was no cute baby robin. Because it was inside the neighbour's cat.

But by chance, or maybe it was not by chance at all, just at that moment I see an inquisitive robin sat outside the coffee shop window. A full bodied, almost round chap with a deep red breast and impossible stick thin legs. He cocks his head at me and blinks. Clearly, he hasn't heard about his young friend yet. I know what to do. The connection is strong enough this time. I think the ring must amplify it somehow. I might not get this chance again. He might take it off and shove it in a drawer. That's what I would do. But he's not me.

But I'm not taking that chance. I'm doing it now and it has to work.

***

Barry rotates the ring on his finger with his thumb, lost in thought, thinking about Phil. His grief seems especially strong today, amplified. He heard a noise at the window and looked up. A robin was tapping its beak on the glass and stopped to cock his head at Barry, fluttering his wings. Having caught his attention, it flew across the street to the Nike store and landed on the illuminated tick sign. A dark shadow passed across the front of the shopfront, in the way that a mist rolls in from the sea. It began to shrink in size, becoming denser. The robin was singing a frantic song and flapped its wings in an agitated manner. The shadow shifted and consolidated further until it formed what was starting to look like the shape of a man. It wasn't like a shadow cast by the sun. Indeed, it was pissing down and there was no sun or artificial light source that would create something like that. It was almost black. Not so much a shadow then, but the complete absence of light. A darknesses. Barry shifted uneasily in his seat. He nervously looked around to see if anyone else was seeing this. His head snapped back to the shadow. To the absence of light. And Barry nearly jumped out of seat when it lifted one dark arm and waved. And then lifted the other arm, flipping him off. Barry laughed out loud, tears springing from his eyes. Phil! He quickly glanced over his shoulder to see if anyone else had noticed what was happening. They hadn't. He sat further forward in his chair and pressed his face close to the window. The shadow started to shift and for a heart stopping moment, he thought that it was going to leave. But it started to move towards him. Shuffling in his seat, afraid to look away or even blink now, Barry watched as it crossed the street with the robin fluttering by its side. It stopped directly in front of the window. Just inches away. Surrounding it was a swirling mist of what looked like grey smoke. As Barry peered deeper into the dark shadow, his nose touching the glass now, he could make out hundreds, no, thousands of twinkling lights from deep inside. It was mesmerising.

Slowly, the twinkling stars became hazy, cloudy. Pulling himself back he focused on the window and noticed that it was wet. He wiped at it with the sleeve of his jumper, but the moisture was on the outside. He could see breath. Actual breath coming from Shadow Phil, causing condensation on the other side of the window. As he starred at it, a handprint appeared. Phil's hand from the other side. Instinctively he lifted his hand and placed it over Phil's, the ring clinking against the glass. Immediately, he was overwhelmed. He almost recoiled, almost pulled his hand away quickly, as if he had touched something scolding hot. But he didn't. Instead, he leaned further into it. He pressed harder with his hand, focussed all of his attention, trying to feel as much as he could. The glass was acting as a conduit between their two realties, only millimetres thick but bridging unfathomable distance. He could hear him, sense his presence. And he understood what Phil wanted, felt the message he was trying to send him. It travelled across space and time and passed through this coffee shop window on a cold, wet October morning. Something went 'ping' inside of Barry's soul. Something that was gripped very hard, or coiled very tight, was blissfully released.

***

That was the most intense experience of my life. Or death. Both, actually. It was indescribable. I was right there, looking right at him. I could see in his eyes that he knew it was me. That I'd come back. There was elation and wonder in those eyes but also resignation and understanding. All the time I spent in the dark place was building up to this. Building up to an opportunity to tell him that it is ok. I am ok. He will be ok. And now it's done. Barry can have peace and move on with his life, and maybe stop moping around his apartment and this crappy coffee shop. Get out there and live his life, get laid, laugh, cry. I know that's what I would do. What I want to do. But I think my time here is coming to an end. Barry's image is starting to fade and although I'm pressing my hand harder against the window, trying to hold on, I know it's no use. I feel the light fading and I'm back in the dark place. But its ok. I've made peace and Barry is going to be ok. I'm dead and that's ok too. It's all ok. All good. I'm fine with it. I am ready. Let the darkness descend. Let oblivion wash over me like a black wave. I'm ready. I said, *I'm ready*.......

........ok, that's embarrassing. I'm still here. I thought that was it. I got all deep and shit and said my last words and everything. Fucking hell, don't tell me this is it now. Stuck in this dark nothingness for all eternity. I don't even have a dick to play with to pass the time. Oh wait, what's that? I see a tiny bright light. There's no sense of perspective in here so I can't tell if it's a large light that is very far away, or a tiny light right in front of my face. It starts to get bigger. Or maybe just closer? Lost in this thought, I start to feel warmth. A surge of incoming temperature in a place that has none of its own. It's getting brighter now, incredibly bright. If I had eyes, I'd lift my hand to shield them. If I had hands. Then it speeds up, is upon me all at once. The light and the warmth envelop me, and I'm filled with a sense of euphoria and understanding. The darkness flashes to white, I feel a wave of energy, a surge of speed and then........

3 Adam & E-5

Nothing, nothing at all. Adam refreshed the display in vain, hoping for a different reading. But he was, apparently, surrounded by nothing. Well, nothing inhabitable anyway. For as far as his scanners could reach there wasn't a single planet that had the correct set of conditions to support any kind of humanoid life. And even if there was something just outside scanner range, and in the direction he was (blindly) travelling in, that would put him at least thirty days out. That's thirty on top of the ninety he'd already been scouring the expanse. Adam let out a sigh from deep inside as he slumped back in his chair and stared at the ceiling. A gentle breeze of stale, recycled air came from the vent above. The lazy, whooshing sound it made was almost deafening in the silence. He could hear himself breathe. The absence of sound mirrored the expanse he was surrounded by, and he felt a sense of panic rising in his chest. Light years of uninterrupted space. Above, below and all around. The enormity of it was overwhelming; he could travel at full speed in this research shuttle for the remainder of his life and relatively speaking, barely move at all.

His holographic dashboard popped up before him, beamed from the tiny implant on his temple. It was amber, alerting him to the fact that he'd been awake for 18 hours and was due a sleep cycle. In the absence of actual day and night, it was important to maintain the illusion of both for physical and mental health. The shuttle's environmental systems begun simulating their night-time cycle. Lights were dimmed, air temperature reduced, and false stars were projected onto the darkened ceilings. Cicada sounds were emitted from the shuttles sound systems. It was intended to be comforting and familiar, to put you at ease while travelling far from home.

He pushed himself away from the console, his chair carrying him to the centre of the flight deck before coming to a stop. "Computer, set navigation to night mode", he said lazily as he walked to the transporter. Standing on the elevated disc, he said, "Computer, my quarters". He felt a short vibration travelling up his body and with a flash of light and a brief tingling sensation, he was in his room. Adam completed his evening ritual. He stripped off his uniform and passed it through the sonic washing machine. He showered, air dried and slipped into the dressing gown he'd packed from home. It was brown and fluffy with worn patches here and there. It was outsized and made him look like a slightly ridiculous, saggy bear, but he didn't care. There was no-one here to see it and anyway, it reminded him of home. Of his apartment in San Francisco, with its rickety wooden steps up from the street. Adam was a sucker for nostalgia, with a particular penchant for late 1970's kitsch. And so he'd scoured the local thrift stores, spent hours on Ebay searching for items to help transport his tiny one bed apartment into a 1970's San Franciscan time capsule. It was awash with orange plastic, tie-dyed fabric and gaudy memorabilia. How he yearned for it all now. It seemed like a million miles away. Actually, Adam thought, a million miles doesn't seem so far away right now. Lost in reminiscing, he scrolled through the replicator menu. More and more options were greyed out now. His mission had only been expected to last thirty days. The replicators were loaded with far more material than was necessary for the mission, as a contingency. And there were emergency rations too. But they would only last so long. Every time another option greyed out and became unavailable, Adam's anxiety grew.

Selecting boiled chicken and rice, a meal which used relatively little replicator material, he slumped into the chair. He ate, watched re-runs of his favourite TV show, drank and fell asleep with the food tray on his chest. A restless, fretful sleep filled with trippy dreams that weren't quite nightmares.

Adam woke with a start to an alarm. He jumped from his sleep, sending the tray crashing to the floor. He flew up from his seat, disorientated. His holographic display was signalling an alert from the flight deck. Silencing it and still in his gown, he transported himself there. Adam navigated the controls to see what had triggered the alarm. His heart raced. Long range sensors had picked something up. A planet. A planet in the middle of nowhere. Well, not quite nowhere. But right on the edge of a small solar system, a very long way away. Looking at the data, Adam couldn't understand why the scans had positively identified this planet. It was too far out from its sun and would be far too cold to support humanoid life. It wasn't showing any of the natural compounds or gasses that he'd programmed into the search criteria either. But the readings showed something odd. They were picking up faint traces of radiation consistent with advanced technology. Radio waves. Sound waves even. Materials that were not consistent with the typology of the planet, suggesting that they didn't originate from there. Which meant that they had been taken there. Adam's mind raced with possible explanations. The scanners weren't picking up any life forms, but the presence of technology and non-indigenous material suggested that something had been there. And the radiation readings suggested that it still might be. If there had been other options, if Adam's situation hadn't started to become quite so desperate, he would probably have dismissed this search result and kept looking. But he couldn't shake the feeling that he was all alone, and that no one was coming for him. His mother ship and crew had been ripped apart by a black hole while he was on a research mission. No one was sending a rescue party all this way just for him. He was presumed lost. Unless he found a way out of this for himself, he would spend what time he had left aimlessly searching, looking, and slowly losing his mind. So, he made a decision based on necessity and the absence of better options. Plotting a course for what the computer referred to as Planet B-112-F97, he sat back in his chair, his mind reeling. The computer estimated the journey to take approximately thirty-three days. Just yesterday, that seemed like an interminable amount of time. But now? With the potential for what he might find on B-112-F97, it seemed like hardly any time at all.

***

E-5 received a proximity alert. Something was approaching, and at speed. Still days away, but almost certainly on a trajectory. Analysing the signal, he identified it as coming from a research shuttle manufactured on Earth. It was a long way from home.

He scanned a wider area and could not detect the presence of a mother ship. It was still too far away for him to be able to detect life signs. The ships signature did not cross check against the BCC (Barbary Colonisation Company) database either. So who or whatever it was, it wasn't a salvage mission. Not that there was much chance of that anyway. E-5 made about a billion calculations, ran a few thousand possible scenarios in just a split second and concluded nothing. The only option open to him was to prepare for the shuttles arrival and wait. And so he slipped back into low energy standby mode. And waited.

***

Adam transported himself from the shuttle to the planet surface. It wasn't the first time that he'd stood on the surface of a planet that wasn't Earth. But it was the farthest he'd been. By a long way. Adam's space suit compensated for temperature, breathable air and gravity as the conditions here were pretty hostile for human physiology. But that, he understood from E-5, had been one of the reasons that this particular planet had been selected. He had entered comms range with B-112-F97 three days before arriving. E-5 had established contact first, sending Adam a standard initiation greeting. After identifying Adam and establishing that he wasn't a hostile threat, E-5 explained his presence on the planet.

About ten years ago, the Barbary Colonisation Company sent a team of engineers and scientists on a mission to a far-flung planet to look at the colonisation practicalities of hostile planets. The technology required to inhabit nearby planets with Earth-like conditions had been around for a while, so the market was pretty saturated. The cutting-edge technology was now in more challenging environments that were further away, and with less natural resources.

And so a team of twenty pioneers had been sent to B-112-F97 on a long-term mission to create a sustainable area, capable of supporting human life for a community of one hundred settlers. It was intended to be self-sufficient and self-maintaining so that minimal support was needed from Earth. The ship that the crew arrived on was designed to be disassembled on arrival, providing building materials. The team set up the perimeter and zoned the initial occupancy area. Pylons were built hundreds of feet into the air in a square formation. Using renewable energy supplied from the planets core, an electric field was created, forming an artificial atmosphere. Gasses were pumped into the newly created bio cube. Flora and fauna from Earth were introduced. Vast quantities of water were released, and artificial weather cycles were initiated. In essence, an Earth-like ecosystem was artificially created in an area about two miles square. Once created, it could sustain itself with little intervention. And against a lot of odds, it was a resounding success. It was testament to the incredible skill and ability of the scientists and engineers on the mission rather than a success for Barbary Colonisation Corporation itself. The latter, it transpired someway during the mission, had borrowed funds from multiple sources in order to finance the project. Having overextended themselves the company had no choice but to liquidate in order to pay off its creditors. The planned consignment of settlers was never sent and therefore the ship that they would have arrived on wasn't available for the science team's return journey to Earth. The cost of retrieving the crew and equipment from B-112-F97 was astronomic and beyond the current financial capabilities of the BCC. While its directors pointed fingers and shirked responsibilities, a previously unscreened virus penetrated the biocube and wiped the science team out in a matter of weeks; they had worked day and night to develop a vaccine and cure for the virus, but it was a race against time, and they lost.

Shortly after, BCC folded, the project was scrapped and the whole thing was forgotten. The creditors took the reports sent back to BCC by the on-planet team and sold the technology for indecent amounts of money. But what was actually built on B-112-F97 was of little interest or use. The cost and time it took to get there was prohibitive. And there was the virus, after all. E-5, the mission's cyborg facilitator, was left alone on a planet light years from Earth with no remaining purpose, other than to complete work on the vaccine, recycle the deceased team for natural resources and play caretaker to an ecosystem that was designed not to need a one.

Upon hearing this, Adam almost turned his ship around. What was the point? The radiation readings, radio waves and presence of technology had all lead him to believe that there might be intelligent life here. Humanoid life. But he'd been mistaken. It was an unpopulated, inhospitable planet save for an area two miles square. And a fucking cyborg. If he kept searching, at least there was hope that he might find something. Some*one*. But here? There was no-one. And thanks to the collapse of BCC, there wasn't going to be either.

But it didn't take Adam long to consider the possibility that this may in fact be his best option. His only option. His shuttle was fairly self-sufficient and equipped with the materials needed to make routine repairs, but it wasn't designed to travel across lightyears of space. It was a research shuttle, short range, medium at a stretch. Without regular docking to a mother ship or a service station, something would eventually fail, and he would be stranded. That's assuming his food supply didn't run out first. And so he had decided to continue to B-112-F97 and check it out for himself.

Adam took in the baron, desolate landscape. It was completely flat, for as far as the eye could see. The soil appeared to have the texture of coarse sand, was dark brown in colour and had a metallic sheen. The dim sun was setting on the horizon, creating an eerie grey light. It reflected off the metallic soil, causing it to sparkle gently. It was almost pretty. Just to the right of where Adam had landed was the biocube. It was an impressive structure. Against such a flat, uninterrupted landscape, the biocube had the appearance of having just popped into existence from nowhere. It looked alien to its surroundings, which of course, it was. The electrical field that contained the artificial atmosphere shimmered and shifted slightly, as it reflected the sunlight. Save for a blueish tint, it was transparent. From this angle all Adam could see inside were trees. Lots of trees. A forest, densely packed and lush green. He was in awe.

"Adam, it's good to meet you".

"Oh hey, sorry, I was just checking out the biocube. Its incredible. Sorry, I'm Adam" He extended his hand in a gesture of goodwill. E-5 took it and gave him a very authentic handshake. Adam was surprised. As a cyborg facilitator to a colonisation mission, he'd expected him to be equipped with the minimum of humanoid feature packs. But they'd splashed out. If he'd passed you in the street, you'd probably not clock him as cyborg at all. That can't have come cheap, Adam thought. They really spared no expense on this mission. No wonder they went bust.

"First things first, this is going to sting a little". E-5 pushed a needle through the medication port of Adam's suit. "Vaccine for the virus. I've since developed the cure, but my analysis shows that it's likely to have gastrointestinal....side effects. You're better off with the vaccine if eating solid food is something that's important to you".

Was E-5 cracking a joke, Adam thought? "Ugh, Ok. I'll take the vaccine please". E-5 was right, it did sting.

"Right you are", said E-5 breezily. "Ok, it works instantly so let's get you inside, and out of that suit".

Inside the decontamination chamber, Adam stripped off his suit and everything he wore underneath. He put his hands above his head and turned slowly as he was blasted with decontaminating gasses. He caught E-5 getting a good look at his junk as he handed Adam some fresh clothes. "My face is up here", Adam joked as he pulled on the pants. E-5 looked up. "Sorry, I've been alone out here for such a long time. I'm only humanoid". Ok, that was definitely a joke, Adam thought. He laughed out loud and realised that he couldn't remember the last time he'd done that. It felt good.

"Hey, are you programmed for that? To have.... feelings?"

E-5 nodded enthusiastically. "Yes, most definitely. My primary function is to aid my human assignees in all areas. On long term missions like this one, that can take on a whole range of meanings. When you put humans together on a planet far from home, they sometimes need an outlet for things they might not want to do with work colleagues. So I help with that too. Guys, girls, I don't mind. I am completely anatomically correct for both sexes. I would imagine that you might have some needs of your own, spending all that time in space alone. After I've shown you around, I'd be happy to...." Adam blushed, despite himself. "No, no – you're ok! Jesus. Come on strong much?!" E-5 hesitated slightly, paused. He faltered a little and looked embarrassed. "Hey, sorry E-5. You didn't do anything wrong. I just like to get to know a guy first". He winked playfully at E-5, who instantly brightened. "Oh, ok - that's fine. Not a problem. It's logged" he said as he tapped his head and made a mechanical, robotic gesture. Adam smiled, despite himself. He couldn't help but warm a little to this pile of advanced mechanics and computer wizardry.

And so E-5 gave him the tour. It was staggering. Adam was seriously impressed at what they had achieved here. The biocube was zoned into distinct areas. The forest, he had already seen. There was a residential zone with pod homes of varying sizes and styles, arranged around a communal recreation area with a coffee shop, a park, a gym and a small town hall. Then there was the work zone, housing various laboratories for scientific research. There was the nursery, where flora and fauna samples bought from earth were grown for release into the biocube. And there was the maintenance area, housing the energy pump, burrowing deep into the planets core, powering the generators, the gravity simulator and the atmosphere generator. The place was incredible.

"This place, E-5. It's unbelievable. That this could be created so far from home. It's tragic that the guys who built it never really saw it in its maturity. And you've maintained this all by yourself? For all these years?"

"Well, yes. I have the advantage that I don't need to rest or sleep. I charge wirelessly and continuously and so I can pretty much keep working with just a maintenance dock every ten days or so. And without the research team here, the place is low maintenance. It runs itself to a large extent. It's how it was designed. I just need to keep all the tech running".

"Does it get lonely? *Can* you get lonely?"

"Yes, a little. I get some pleasure from feeding the birds and watching things grow. But I'm programmed to be sociable and interactive. It's been hard".

They arrived back where they had started – at the residential zone. They stopped outside a small pod home, coloured sky blue with round windows. A beautiful cherry blossom tree bloomed by the front door. A hummingbird busied itself with pollen as Adam took in the scene and sighed contentedly.

"This", E-5 pointed to the house Adam was looking at, "this could be your home. If you wanted it. You could stay".

"Huh? What?". Adam had been lost in a thought that he couldn't quite bring into focus. "Live here?"

E-5 paused a second, as if considering something. "Well, you can certainly rest here for tonight at least. Regroup. Consider your options. You've only just arrived, and you'll be far more comfortable here, in this fully featured and fully furnished house, than back on your shuttle".

It made some sense. To be on terra firma for a few days seemed very appealing and he needed to get his head together, to think about what he was going to do next. E-5 seemed to sense that a decision was in the balance. "Just stay for tonight and see how you feel tomorrow. I'll even cook you dinner. I make a believable lasagne. I've got an interesting recipe for synthesised beef".

And that's just what happened. Adam stayed the night. And the next morning he decided to stay just one more night. He needed a little more time. But he made that same decision each morning until before he knew it, he'd lost track of the days. He'd tried very hard not to fall in love with the sky-blue pod home from the moment he stepped inside. Tried very hard not to appreciate the quirky, future – retro design. To ignore the fact that the bed was the most comfortable he had ever slept in. To not get too attached to the hummingbird that visited his back yard and was now so tame, that Adam literally had her eating out of his hand. Certainly, he wouldn't name her, he promised to himself (she was called DeDe). He tried not to while away so many hours sitting on the back porch swing with E-5, bonding over their differences. Tried not to fall slightly in love with his strange mix of robotic accuracy and absoluteness, charmingly offset by the occasional glimpse of something resembling humanity, vulnerability. But Adam pretty much failed at all of it. Despite himself, he was becoming very comfortable in this idyllic, two square miles of paradise. He'd have thought it claustrophobic, but strangely it wasn't. Instead, it felt comfortable, cosy and manageable. His whole world was contained in this neat little package and for a time, he didn't need to think or worry about anything else. But of course, he did. This couldn't last, he would need more, eventually. He would miss *people*. People other than E-5. Friends, family, a stranger in a bar. There was none of that here. And there never would be. And the longer he stayed, the harder it would be to leave. The thought had been gnawing away at him, and each day it became harder to ignore, harder to push to the back of his mind. But there came a time where it could be ignored no longer.

Adam was preparing dinner one evening while E-5 was updating him on the daily comings and goings of the cube. The atmosphere gas mix was 0.0001% out of synch – he'd fixed it. The weather system was about to cycle to rain – they should bring in the bean bags from the back yard. He'd planted some new flowers in the remembrance garden that he'd grown from the seed bank. Adam listened distractedly, trying to ignore the elephant in the room. And all at once, it was too much.

"E-5 – just STOP! Just stop". He put down the spatula and turned off the hob. "E-5, we need to talk".

E-5 looked confused. He tilted his head to the side and regarded Adam, taking in his body language, scanning for blood pressure and a thermal reading. "Adam, you're stressed. You're feeling anxiety. Is it the sauce?"

"No E-5, it's not the sauce". Adam sighed and sat down next to him, putting a hand on his thigh and giving it a gentle squeeze. E-5 looked down at it, then looked up at Adam with an expression of concern.

"E. What is this we are doing here? What's this game that we're playing?"

"Game, Adam? I wasn't aware that we were playing a game. What are the rules?"

Adam's heart melted a little. "No, E, I mean, what are we doing on this planet. Together. What's our game plan. Sorry, what's our long-term objective? I've been thinking about it a lot. In many ways I'm so happy here, happy here with you. I've grown fond of you in a way I never thought I would. Or could. You're special to me E, this place is special to me, and there is part of me that wants it to stay like this forever".

"But it can't?"

"No, I'm not sure it can E. I need more. I don't know that I can spend the rest of my life, all those years with just these square two miles and only you for company. For conversation. For family. For friendship. For sex. For everything. It's not enough. It won't be enough. I need more. Humans need more".

"So you want to leave, is that what you are saying? You want to leave and try to get back to Earth. Or find another humanoid civilisation? Have you got any idea what the odds of that happening are? Of finding either of those two things, equipped with just your vessel and a human life span? I could tell you the odds of that happening if you like. Let's just say they're slim, Adam".

"I know E, I know. But I feel that I have to try. I just can't imagine this being all there is for the next 70 odd years". Adam moved his chair closer to E, putting their foreheads together. "But I can't imagine leaving you either. I need you too".

"But I must remain here Adam, you know that. It's my programming. I'm not to abandon this settlement under any circumstances. I can't go against that. It's not that I won't, I just can't".

"I could kidnap you in the night and steel you away on my vessel" Adam joked, giving E-5 a conspiratorial wink".

E-5 put his hand on Adam's thigh now and squeezed back his reply. Adam sighed, slumping his shoulders in resignation. They sat like that together for a while until E-5 suddenly shifted in his seat, looking uncomfortable. Adam glanced up. His face was twitching, the muscles around his mouth and eyes contorting spasmodically. "E, what is it? What's wrong?" He looked agitated, conflicted.

"Adam, I have something to tell you that may be relevant. That may have a bearing on your decision. I haven't told you until now because it's classified information that I'm not permitted to share. But I've wrestled with my systems and found a loophole in the programming".

"Okaaaayyyy" said Adam, tentatively.

E-5 took Adam's hands in his and looked straight into Adam's eyes when he spoke. "The original colonisation mission's brief was just to set up the biocube. But before they got the virus, the team built a fertility lab and started harvesting their sperm and eggs for storage. Kind of like an insurance policy for if something went wrong with the mission, so that if there were to be some kind of disaster that wiped out most of the team, and if there was no way of getting back to earth, they could at least start repopulating".

"Wait, so there's the genetic material and the technology here to... create life?! To build a population?!"

"Yes, most definitely. Under different circumstances I might have begun the process myself. But it's against my coding. Some hysterical nonsense about cyborgs plotting for world domination. We are hard coded not to autonomously interfere in either the procreation of the human race or in the production or advancement of cyborg technology. But you, you could........*we* could............"

"Wait, I know where you're going with this. But that's, that's.....I don't know. But we can't. I can't. I'd be playing God. We'd be playing God".

"Ha, 'God'! I hadn't thought about it like that. But you're right. But rather I think the scientists and engineers that built this place would be God in this scenario. I think you and I would be more like Adam and Eve. We've been given this place, this paradise. This perfect, unspoilt haven where there is no good, and no bad. It's up to us what we do with it. It *could* be up to us. Man and machine, building a civilisation together. Starting from scratch. No inherited social norms. No preconceptions of hierarchy, race, gender or humanity. The possibilities are endless. What you would spend the rest of your natural life searching for in the expanse, we could build right here, on B-112-F97".

It was too much. This was too much. It was preposterous. Wrong. Unethical. Wasn't it? But then, Adam countered, it was *possible.* They *could* do it. Man's underlying instinct is to survive. To Procreate. To advance. Maybe born out of a series of unfortunate and tragic events, Adam's and E-5's presence here, in this place, was a springboard for humanity. A chance to leapfrog human / cyborg evolution into the future. Man, and machine. In harmony. Adam's mind raced. What if being marooned in deep space and ending up here with E-5 wasn't such a cluster fuck after all. What if this was exactly where he was supposed to be? What if everything he had ever done was leading up to this. To be here. To this opportunity; Adam & E-5 and their own version of.....

Adam took in a deep breath and held it for the longest time. He was at a crossroads and taking either path would be life changing. Thinking that he would never be able to make the decision, he just did. Something clicked in his brain, and it all became suddenly very clear.

"Well," said Adam finally. "The first thing we'd have to do is give this place a new name. What we are going to do here, what we are going to create here can't be referred to as 'B-112-F97'. So how do you feel about……."

4 Annie Walker

I breeze into being. I shimmer into existence. Briefly, intangible. A wisp of air, a shard of light, a subtle change of temperature. I arrive anywhere and everywhere, exactly where I am meant to be but entirely without volition.

I see an old lady, sipping tea carefully from a cracked, china cup. Sat upright in a high-backed chair with lace doilies on the arms, she is proud, proper. She is dressed in worn clothes, carefully looked after as they were once expensive. Alone in her modest flat, she is surrounded by the bric a brac of her life. A life that has seen two husbands; one lost to war and the other to cancer. A life that has seen her as daughter, sister, wife, grandmother, widow and although there is not a living soul that knows it, a mistress. But I know. I know it all.

Surrounded by the artefacts of her life, a pharaoh in her tomb, she tries to hold still her treacherous, shaky hand which threatens to spill her tea.

I sense that she is expecting me, dressed in her finest clothes, sat in her good chair and drinking from her finest china. Her patent leather handbag rests on the carpet by her side. Swollen feet are stuffed into tight shoes. Tan tights are bunched and puckered at the ankles, and I know that this would upset her, this imperfection. But it does not matter now. She understands that.

I wait patiently. I use the time to get a sense of Annie Walker before it is time to act. Each visitation is personal and unique. I move in closer, drawing myself down to eye level, just inches from her face. She cannot see me, not yet. I peer deep into misty blue eyes, and beyond. This is a very old soul. And one that I have visited several times before. There have been other custodians before Annie Walker. But at the age of ninety-seven, she is the longest serving. She would take pride in that, I am sure.

And all at once, it is time. I sense it coming, just moments before she does. I pull back and ready myself. I begin the process of manifestation. It takes considerable energy and concentration. I watch Annie's face as a ripple of pain twitches at the corner of her lips and passes across her brow. It is her heart. I can feel it now. It is not a bad way to go. It will be quick, and she will be gone before she knows what is happening. She will not suffer.

At that, the ripple turns into a surging tsunami. A fast, urgent, lethal wave of pain. Her hand instinctively releases the cup and saucer, sending it crashing to the floor as she clutches her chest. She lurches forward. I watch her body hit the carpet as I lean in to catch her soul.

She slumps for a moment in my arms, not moving. I wait patiently. When she begins to stir, I help her to her feet. Leaving a body after so many years is disorientating. I take her hands in mine. We are both ethereal now, energy as old as time. I can feel everywhere that she has been, everyone she has loved, all that she has had and all that she has lost. She looks up at me, eyes no longer misty but bright, sparkling azure. She is full of questions.

"It is alright", I assure her. "You will not remember yet, but we have met before. Many lifetimes ago. You have nothing to fear from me. You have nothing to fear at all. I am here to take you home, Annie Walker". She opens her mouth as if to ask a question, but I silence it with a smile. "You will understand, you will remember."

I draw myself up to full height and extend my large wings outward. I pull them forward to envelop Annie, combining our energy. Without flashing lights, without puffs of smoke and without any theatrics at all, we are gone.

5 Shooter In The Park

It is a warm, spring morning. The sky is dazzling blue, the air is crisp. Trees are budding. Fresh, green shoots emerge from warmed soil. Birds busy themselves noisily with the gathering of materials for nests. Winter's pallet of browns and auburn hues make way for green, pink, yellow and blue in pastel shades. There is an energy in the air, the promise of something new.

The park is busy with all manner of people, going about their lives. Joggers, some serious with real sweat and worn trainers while others simply pose, pristine with coiffured hair and designer sportswear. New parents are relieved to get their kids outside, as they run and shout in the open air. A dog walker tries to regain control as her excitable pack pulls her along at speed. Young lovers walk hand in hand, arm in arm. The air around them is charmed, gilded. Their infatuation, a love that has no limits, a love that can conquer all. This is my obsession. My fascination. A love that is untested and is therefore pure and innocent. It emanates from them, a perfume. Passers-by can almost smell it. Some smile, warmly; knowingly. Others scowl, cynically; jaded.

I feel the weight of the quiver resting on my hip, freshly loaded with arrows. Each one is marked for someone. I creep through the undergrowth, peer from behind trees. It isn't strictly necessary; people don't really see anything these days, they are far too preoccupied with themselves. But I like the hunt, I enjoy the game. I position myself behind a large bush overlooking the lake, and I wait. I hold my bow in my left hand. I squeeze the grip hard to relieve some of the tension I'm feeling. With my right hand I gently caress the sharp tip of an arrow, play with the serrated edge against the side of my thumb. I try to steady my breath, regulate my heartbeat. I wait patiently.

Some kids pass by on scooters. A few joggers. A man strays from the path, looking nervously around him as he walks towards the bush I am using for cover. To my horror, he unzips and relieves himself in front of me. He doesn't see me. He is too busy looking around for anyone coming up the path. He scurries away and I try to ignore the smell of urine. Try to stop it from ruining the moment, the thrill of the hunt. An elderly lady passes by. Slowly. The shopping trolley she pulls along behind her has a squeaky wheel. I can hear it long after she turns the corner of the path, away from the lake. I am distracted by it for a moment. I almost miss the scruffy college student skulking his way along the path. He is tall and thin, with a sickly pallor. His head is hung low, long hair covering his face. He is hunched forward, lost in his phone. His steps are heavy and deliberate, each one a seemingly monumental effort. He is too young to be carrying so much weight on his shoulders, to be so cynical. You see, I know him without ever having met him. It's a gift. A superpower, if you like. Disillusioned with the world, he lives a virtual existence. He feels that no one understands him, that no one 'gets' him. He has watched too much Netflix and played too much Xbox. Has spent too much time texting, Snapchatting, Instagramming, Facebooking, anything that doesn't require him to physically engage. All his skills are virtual. He's lost the ability to connect with the real world. It's a common affliction these days. And so he doesn't appreciate that he is living in a safe city, walking through a beautifully landscaped public park on a warm, spring morning. He doesn't notice that birds are singing, flowers are beginning to bloom, that there is life and hope and possibility all around him. Maybe I should intervene. Maybe I should make him put down that phone and look up. Look up and really see something. Someone. My index finger taps the tip of each arrow in my quiver, testing for the correct one. The correct one for him. I find it. I press my fingertip against the head until it pricks the skin, leaving a little of my blood on it. I reach for the arrow shaft and then I see her. I see her walking brightly along the same path but from the opposite direction, towards him. I know her too. I like her. She is bright, she is bubbly, she walks as if on a cushion of air. She wears a floaty floral dress that billows and sashays as she strides carefree along the path in strappy sandals. She carries a small bunch of wildflowers in her hand, picked from the side of the road. Not much more than weeds really, but she sees beauty in them. She holds them up to her face happily, takes in their aroma and smiles broadly. A robin jumps down to a low hanging branch along the path, and she stops to look at him. Stops to listen to his cheerful song. She is sunny and bright and epitomises the season. And just like that, I make her my target too. They are night and day, but that's what makes it so perfect. That's what will make it so satisfying. I must move fast as she will soon be upon him. My finger dances again across the arrows before finding hers, finger pricked, blood deposited.

    I nock her arrow first. I take a deep breath and raise the bow to my target, drawing back the string. It creaks under the pressure and the sound excites me, thrills me. I see the tip of the arrow gleaming in the sunlight. I track her progress along the path, following her with my aim. As the path turns towards me, her chest is exposed and I release her arrow, sending it ripping through the air and into her chirpy little heart. All in the same breath, I quickly draw his arrow and take aim. I pause, steady my shaking arm and just as he approaches the same turn on the path, I send his arrow soaring into the spring air. I release the breath that I have been holding and feel the tension melt away from my body as I watch the scene play out in front of me.

***

Sam and Bella turn to face one another, staring deeply into each other's eyes. Wide, goofy smiles spread across each of their faces. Both hearts surge with happiness on this special day as tears prick at their eyes; neither are confident of getting through their vows without crying. They give each other a knowing look as Sam takes Bella's hands in his, feeling her familiar warmth. The wedding guests laugh gamely as he jumps the gun and steals a kiss. The minister coughs for effect, restoring order as the service begins.

It's been exactly a year since that fateful day in the park. They had been opposites in so many ways. Living such different lives. So little in common on the face of things, but at a deeper, more fundamental level, soul mates waiting to connect. Both were derailed that day from the separate tracks they had been travelling on. From the moment they laid eyes on each other, the attraction was instant. Undeniable. They had both felt it. Both had been thunderstruck. Neither could take their eyes off the other. Neither could understand what was happening to them, why they fell so hard and so quickly. But they knew, they could feel that something had……clicked into place that day. Call it destiny, fate, kismet; call it want you want. In the same way you know the sun will rise, that day follows night, both Sam & Bella knew that they were destined to meet on that day, that they would be together for every subsequent day, and for the rest of their lives.

***

I watch from the back of the church, peering out from behind a column. My heart is bursting with joy. I am so happy. I knew they would be perfect for each other. Sometimes it's a risk, sometimes you never quite know if the match will stick. My arrows are powerful, but external influences can still blow my work off course. But these two; I just knew. I habitually survey the gathering, cast my eye over the celebrants while passing a hand across the arrow heads, searching for a feeling, a potential match. But I bring myself back into the moment. No, for today this is enough.

6 The Bad Lamp

Cole Lovett has not a friend in the world. He is as miserable and as cynical as it is possible for a man to be. He is without kindness, without compassion and without conscience. He looks out for himself and his best interests in every situation and anyone that gets in his way, is collateral damage. He carries around with him a sense of entitlement that is becoming all too common today. And because the good life that he feels entitled to has not fallen from the sky into his lap, he is resentful and indignant.

Yes, he had his fair share of hard knocks growing up, it is true. But many have had it harder and were offered fewer opportunities to turn their lives around. Every piece of good fortune that comes his way, he squanders. Every act of goodwill extended to him is snatched, used up and spat out.

Cole Lovett is a bad apple, and you should not feel sorry for him. He has it coming. You do not see it yet, but you will.

***

On the evening of Cole Lovett's reckoning, he walks home from work. His footsteps are heavy, and angry. An altercation with a co-worker just before clocking out has left him in a foul mood. Head down and shoulders hunched against the driving rain, he curses and mutters a stream of obscenities under his breath, only pausing to stuff another bite of kebab into his mouth. He chews sloppily with his mouth open, food falling to the pavement. He stops in a doorway to take shelter. Looking down, he sees a man in a sleeping bag, surrounded by cardboard and tin foil. He looks up at Cole, then at the kebab, then back at Cole, hungrily. Cole pauses before extending his arm, offering the last of the kebab. Surprised, the man shuffles position in order to reach out and take it, but just before he does, Cole pulls back his arm and makes a show of stuffing what is left of the kebab greedily into his mouth. It doesn't all fit and so some of it falls to the floor by his feet. The homeless man scrambles to pick up the fallen pieces as Cole snorts, a cruel smile twitching at the corner of his greasy mouth. He scrunches up the wrapper and drops it to the ground before belching loudly and walking away.

He turns the corner, crosses the road and heads down the busy high street. Neon signs reflect in deep, wide puddles. People dash into shops to take cover from the rain or dash out of them into waiting taxis and buses. The air is close and filled with the sound of tyres rushing through standing water. Cole feels a burning sensation in his chest and rubs it instinctively. 'Those fucking Turks and their cheap-shit kebabs' he curses, as he heads into the chemist for some indigestion tablets. Cole pulls down his hood as he searches out the right aisle. Picking the cheapest brand he can find, he makes his way to the till. The queue is long, and Cole lets out a loud, frustrated groan. "For fucks sake" he cries, loud enough for the cashier to hear. The elderly gentleman ahead of him turns around to give him a disapproving look. Cole is unrepentant and unembarrassed. "They should open more fucking tills! I've got better things to do with my time than to stand here all day like a fucking idiot." This provokes a raised eyebrow from the gentleman. "You know, young man, there is no need to be quite so foul mouthed. If your time really is so precious, then I suggest you use the self-service till, just over there.' He takes a shaking hand out of a worn pocket and points a bony finger. As he does, a wallet falls from his pocket to the floor. The gentleman turns back around and without a thought, without any deliberation, Cole kicks the wallet to the side and places his right foot over it, in one swift motion. "Yeah, maybe I will, old man" he says mockingly as he kneels to fake-tie his shoe. With a slight of hand, he pockets the wallet. He quickly self-scans and pays for his tablets before leaving the store. He expertly rummages through the wallet, taking the cash and dumping the rest in the bin. He looks back to the store through the window to see the elderly gentleman patting himself down, looking confused and distressed. "Stupid old fucker" he mutters as he heads back into the night.

The rain begins to fall with added resolve in fat, heavy drops. Cole decides to use his windfall to get a taxi, and just as he has the thought, a black cab pulls to the curb. He pulls open the door and climbs in. As he reaches to pull the door closed, he sees a heavily pregnant lady waddling across the pavement towards him. "Hey!" she yells, "that was my taxi!". Cole flashes her a bright, cheerful grin, and chimes "not any more it isn't!" as he pulls the door shut, giving the driver his address. The lady, shocked and appalled, at least has the wherewithal to give him a one finger salute as the taxi pulls away.

***

These latest displays of Cole Lovett's complete disregard for others, for his complete and utter selfishness, confirm to me what I already know. They validate the selection that I have already made. And now you see it too; Cole Lovett really is a bad apple.

***

Cole returns to his lonely, dreary flat. Walking the length of the dimly lit hallway he approaches his front door, 23C. As he draws closer, he sees something unfamiliar, unexpected. Placed squarely on his doormat is…is…he does not know what it is. He slows his pace instinctively and approaches it with caution. Always suspicious, always cynical, he glances over his shoulder. There is nobody there. He turns back to the mysterious object and moves in closer. Bending down, he looks all around it, without touching. He pushes it with his finger, gingerly. It is heavy and substantial. And dirty, crusted with soil as if dug up from the ground. He identifies it as some kind of lamp. It is short and squat, but elegant with an ornately hooked handle and a long, elaborate spout. 'It's a fucking Genie lamp!', Cole exclaims to himself. He picks it up and is surprised at its weight. He looks around once more to confirm that he is alone before quickly entering the flat with his mysterious treasure.

A single naked lightbulb struggles to illuminate the small, dirty space. One room houses the sad existence that is Cole Lovett's life. A tatty sofa is held together with duct tape and doubles up as a bed. A coffee table is littered glass pipes, bottles, scorched foil and lighters. The floor is strewn with takeaway cartons from various establishments. The kitchenette is piled high with dirty plates and cups providing a breeding ground for a myriad of flies. Cole clears a space on the coffee table, carefully places the lamp down and goes in search of cleaning materials. Realising that he doesn't own any, he picks up a dirty shirt from the floor and runs it under the tap. Sitting on the sofa, he picks up the lamp. He carefully dabs it with the wet cloth and removes some of the heavy soiling. He reveals glimpses of gold, jewels and a rush of excitement shoots through him. He cleans away more of the dirt, revealing an inscription running along the length of the spout. It is written in a language that he does not understand, in characters that are unfamiliar to him. In order to see it better, he grabs a sock from under the sofa and buffs the lamp a little.

He starts slowly, rubbing gently in small, circular motions. The lamp becomes warm to the touch. The inscription is clearer now although still unfamiliar to Cole. The gems release a little of their seductive sparkle as they are buffed by the grubby sock. Cole lets out a small giggle, he can hardly believe his luck. His mind runs away with his imagined fortune as he rubs harder, with more vigour. The lamp becomes warmer. It starts to emit a sound now, in the same way that a fine wine glass sings when you rub the rim with a wet finger. It becomes louder as Cole feels the lamp resonate. He is exhilarated, strangely giddy. He is aware that the only thing he wants to do, the only thing that is important in the whole world at this moment, is to continue rubbing the lamp. He feels compelled. Cole's greedy eyes are wide, transfixed. He is bewitched.

And then he notices it. Out of the corner of his eye, Cole sees smoke. Languid, silvery wisps are emanating from the long, ornate spout. He stops buffing. He places the lamp carefully on the table and jumps up, backing away. The lamp continues to sing its high-pitched song and starts to shake a little, causing the lid to rattle. The wisps of smoke come faster now, beginning to gather in the air, consolidating. And then all at once, with a loud swoosh and a change in air pressure that makes Cole's ears pop, the smoke takes form, manifesting itself into the shape of…..Cole is not sure what he is seeing. He is too stunned to process it. Rubbing his eyes, he staggers back in disbelief. And in fear. He sees the figure of a man.

"Fuck me, fuck me, FUCK ME" Cole shouts as he turns and runs for the door.

"Stop right there, Cole Lovett" booms a baritone voice. He stops in his tracks. Frozen. Terrified.

"You do not turn your back on a Genie. Especially THIS Genie." Every hair on Cole's body stands on end as a terrible creeping sensation shoots down his spine. His feet feel nailed to the floor. He is unable to move from this spot, held by an invisible force. He slowly turns around, eyes shut tightly, shoulders hunched and tensed. It is all he can do to open his eyes to a squint and look up at what hangs in the air before him. The head is large, grotesque in comparison to the small body supporting it. He has no arms or legs. His torso is shaped like a fat letter 'S', tapering at each end to a wisp. Cole feels large, penetrating, vibrant green eyes intensely regarding him, looking through him; it is quite terrifying to be the object of their gaze. A disturbingly wide, grinning mouth reminds Cole of the Cheshire cat from Alice in Wonderland. Stretching almost the entire width of his face, there is malice in it.

"What the fuck is this, what are you, how is this happening?" Cole stutters, hating the panicked, squeaky tone of his voice. "This is some kind of trick, some kind of practical joke. I'll fucking kill the fucker who dares to fucking mess with me, I'll……."

"Shut up, Cole. Just shut up. I've seen and heard just about as much from you as I can stand. Any more, and I will lose control and smite you where you stand." His eyes flash angrily. "Do I have to explain the word 'smite' to you, Cole Lovett? I have observed that you have a somewhat limited vocabulary, comprising largely of expletives. Smite is to beat, to smack or to THRASH". His eyes narrow and a malevolence twitches at the corners of his grotesque grin. Cole's fire is quickly extinguished, and he is left feeling small, impotent.

"I will get to the point as I do not wish to spend any more time in your presence than is necessary. I am a Genie; you may have guessed. But I'm not the kind of Genie that you have read about in children's books or seen depicted in popular culture. Those Genies do exist, but you would never be visited by that type of Genie. No, because you are Cole Lovett and the Cole Lovetts of this world get visited by Genies like ME." He puffs out his chest, voice booming.

"You are a bad apple, Cole Lovett. I have been observing you for some time. Watching, assessing. And I have been appalled. You have no respect for anyone, no love for your fellow man. You have repeatedly shown yourself to be selfish, cruel, loveless and despicable. But even after all I have seen, all that you have shown me, I still felt that I should give you one more chance. One more opportunity to show me that somewhere inside of you is a shred of decency, of humanity. And so, this very evening I sent you three tests. Three opportunities to redeem yourself, just a little. And you failed, Cole Lovett. You failed." There was a pregnant pause while the Genie waited for the penny to drop.

"What do you mean, what tests?" Cole thinks quickly, replaying the events of the evening in his mind. "The tramp? And the old fart in the chemist? That's just two! And anyway, I didn't know. That's not fair! If you had warned me, I would have been better, I would have…"

"Warned you?! A good act means nothing if it is carried out in the interest of self-preservation. And the fact that you do not even remember the heavily pregnant lady, the heavily pregnant lady in LABOUR whose taxi you gleeful stole, well, that speaks volumes."

"Wait, I didn't know she was in labour, how could I? I wouldn't have taken the taxi if I'd known!"

"I am not sure that is true, Cole. But it does not matter. This is not a discussion. This is not a negotiation. This is a one-way communication where I tell you what is going to happen, and you listen" Cole started to stammer a protest, but the Genie continued, oblivious. "I am not the kind of Genie that grants wishes. But I am instrumental in making them possible. You see, when a mortal stumbles upon a lamp, rubs it and is visited by a Genie, they typically are granted a wish. But as powerful as we are, Genies are unable to conjure something out of thin air. It may appear that way, but in fact every wish that we grant has a balancing…. transaction, if you will. It is the way of the universe. Every action must have an equal and opposite reaction. Somebody somewhere will find a good lamp and will be granted a wish. And someone like you will find a bad lamp, and what has been wished for, will be taken from you. That is where I come in. My kind scour the earth, looking for suitable subjects, looking for people just like you, Cole Lovett. Lowlifes, criminals, general scum of the earth. To use a modern-day reference that you may understand, think of us of the Robin Hood of wishes. Redistributing wealth, health and privilege to those who deserve it, from those who do not."

The Genie pauses, regarding Cole. He stands dumfounded, slack mouthed and wide eyed. His mind is reeling, trying to make sense of it. He swings from disbelief, to fear, to anger and back to disbelief. "This is crazy, this can't be happening. I'm hallucinating. A delayed reaction to all the drugs and booze. Or a brain tumour, or maybe I'm passed out on the floor, and this is all a bad dream. Yes, that's it. Come on, if you're really a Genie, if they really exist, then do some magic. Do something to prove to me that I'm not dreaming this. Otherwise, I don't buy into it, and you can fuck off." Cole's words may have been bold, but they were betrayed by his shaky voice and trembling body.

"I do not have to prove anything to you, Cole. There is no requirement for me to convince you of a single thing. Believe it or do not. Either way, you entered into a contract when you took the lamp and summoned me. It is done. You are on the hook."

"But what do I have anyway?" Cole tries to reason, "What have I got in my shit-show of a life that anyone would possibly wish for?"

"The fact that you are grateful for nothing, perceive wealth only in material terms and are blind to all the privileges that you have is part of the problem." The Genie drew himself up, reaching the ceiling before baring down on Cole, those dreadful eyes looking directly into his. "The contract is made", he glared, impatiently. "Very shortly, a good lamp will be found, a wish will be granted and what is wished for will be taken from you." Cole blinks, dumbstruck. "And now I will leave you. And you should pray, Cole Lovett, that you never see me again."

Before he can protest the Genie disperses, a final wisp of smoke dancing from the spout like an extinguished match. Cole leaps forward, grabbing the lamp. He shakes it desperately, calling out for the Genie to return. He pulls off the lid and searches inside. He rubs it frantically with his sleeve but of course, nothing happens. He turns it over and examines it again, astonished. What had been reassuringly heavy and opulent is now lightweight and cheap. The rich, indulgent gold is now thin and brassy. The exquisite jewels that had sparkled expensively, are dull and lifeless. Cole looks closer and sees that they are plastic. So obviously plastic! It is just a tacky ornament. Not even that! A child's fucking toy! In a frustrated rage, he hurls it at the wall. He paces around the flat trying to make sense of everything. He sees the lamp on the floor, mocking him. Stamping on it, he cracks it in half. Unsatisfied and with hot tears running down his cheeks, he stamps on the pieces repeatedly, frenziedly, until the lamp is reduced to dozens of tiny plastic shards.

He slumps to the sofa, sobbing, unable to make sense of what has happened, unable to believe it but unable to dismiss it either. He looks around the flat frantically for distraction, something familiar to help ground him. His eyes settle on the stash of drugs on the coffee table. He quickly reaches out for a small white container and pops a couple of benzos, chasing them down with thirsty glugs of Jack Daniels straight from the bottle. He chokes a little and vomits. Searching through regurgitated kebab with his index finger, he finds the two benzos. He puts them back in his mouth and downs the remaining Jack Daniels before dropping the empty bottle to the floor. He lays down on the sofa, closes his eyes and waits for oblivion.

Cole sleeps fretfully for many hours, through to the following afternoon. Drifting in and out of hallucinogenic dreams, he writhes, twitches and sweats profusely, occasionally shouting out in his sleep. When he eventually regains consciousness, he peels himself off the sticky sofa to make noodles. He eats a few mouthfuls and feels nauseous. He moves back to the sofa, pops more benzos and switches from Jack Daniels to Vodka. He passes out again.

The flat is quiet now, the only sound being the hum of the empty fridge. And the flat is dark, very dark. His head aches. Throbs. It feels as if someone is trying to push out his eyes from inside his skull. Unable to see, he pats the sofa with his hands to find his phone. He touches something wet and lumpy. Recoiling quickly, he wipes vomit from his hands onto the rug. He locates his phone, holds it up to wake the screen, but nothing. "Fuck", he mutters. Dead battery. He stands but is lightheaded and disorientated. His legs are weak and trembling. He feels his way around the coffee table, over to the kitchen counter. He pats the wall with his hands until he finds the light switch. Flicks it. But nothing. "Fuck, Fuck, FUCK!!" he shouts in frustration. He feels worse than he has ever felt in his life, like death warmed over, and now he has to deal with the fucking electricity company over a missed payment. He doubles back, using the wall to feel his way to the front door. He squints in anticipation of the bright light from the hallway as he pulls open the door, but it is dark. Cole pauses, confused. "What the...." he mutters, and he gingerly crosses the hall to knock at the door of 18C.

After a short while, the door creaks open and Cole is hit with a waft of hot air and a strong odour of wet dog, turning his fragile stomach. He hears Bob take in a sharp intake of breath.

"Shit, Cole, are you ok? Oh my God, Cole?!"

Annoyed at Bob's fussy, over the top response to just about everything, Cole snaps back. "Bob, just calm the fuck down. It's a power cut. I thought it was just my place, but it must be the whole building."

"Power cut? What are you talking about? Cole, your...."

"Bob! All the lights are out, that's what I'm talking about for fuck's sake! In my place, in the hallway and I can't see any light coming from your flat either! What do you ….."

"Cole, just calm down, ok? You're in shock. Here, take my arm and come inside. I'll call for an ambulance."

Cole's head is still fuzzy from the benzos. Nothing is making any sense.

"Bob, get your corpse-like hand off me. I don't need your fucking help, I….."

"But Cole, your eyes, what…..has happened to…..your eyes?!" Bob rushes inside and Cole hears him call for an ambulance. A terrible, creeping thought begins to work its way to the surface. The drug induced veils of confusion, numbness and disorientation begin to lift. He remembers. The lamp. There is a terrible sinking feeling, the floor falling from beneath him. The Gen…..

His legs give way, and he falls to his knees. He holds his hands in front of his face, unable to see them even at this close range. He finds courage from somewhere deep inside, and steels himself to place quivering hands onto his face. His cheeks are wet and tacky. Sticky with something. He gingerly works his fingers up to his....where his.....eyes......should be. He tentatively feels for them, probing fingers gently tapping around the awful, empty sockets.

7 Ever Decreasing Circles

Ryan caught his breath at the top of the stairs and instinctively checked his pulse. The old wooden banister creaked as he rested his weight against it. Breathless and lightheaded from the exertion, he walked carefully across the hall to his home office, slumping into his chair at the desk. His skin was cold and clammy. His heart was racing impatiently, knocking hard at the inside of his ribs as if desperate to escape a fire in his chest. He took an urgent sip of water from the bottle on the desk and pulled open a drawer, hurriedly searching for the right pills. He was tired. Tired now, tired today, tired generally; of this. A wave of nausea passed over him and he concentrated hard on regulating his breath. He visualised snow peaked mountains and crystal-clear waters. Alpine fresh air and tall green spruces. His heart settled, the hard hammering abating to a relenting thud. The nausea subsided. He slammed the drawer shut in frustration as he felt an angry, hot tear roll down his cheek.

Ryan felt that he deserved this, that it was karma for the life he had lived. A lazy, greedy and selfish life. He had consumed relentlessly. Eaten up all that life had to offer. And when it hadn't been offered to him, he had pushed in and taken it anyway. He had found success in his career by becoming an expert in doing just enough to get by while diligently exploiting others in order to get ahead. He'd burned so many bridges along the way that he was surrounded by a team of subordinates who would cheerfully stab him in the back at the first opportunity.

He was lonely in his private life too, overcompensating for insecurities with vulgar displays of wealth, possession and status. With incredibly low self-worth inherited from a bullying father and a cold mother, he felt that it is was all he had to offer. He surrounded himself with the best of everything that he could afford. Anything that glittered in an effort to dazzle the people around him, distract them with smoke and mirrors from the fact that he was empty inside.

But when no-one was looking, food was his comfort. It was what Ryan used to dazzle and distract himself, from himself. And all the wrong food; anything processed, and everything fast. At his worst, he had been known to stop at Domino's Pizza after work, eat one large pizza on the drive home and the other sat on the sofa, watching Netflix. Along with fries, cheesecake and a six pack, he would chain-smoke his way through his second pack of cigarettes of the day before passing out.

Ryan wiped the hot tear from his cheek and blinked hard. He tried to blink away the dark thoughts and demons that were always lurking at the edges of his thoughts. He caught his reflection in the iMac Pro's enormous screen. He looked terrible. Old beyond his years, and tired. His faced was gaunt as a result of the weight that he had lost. Grey skin sagged, having lost its elasticity. Cheekbones, submerged under layers of fat for decades were now raised to the surface like an old shipwreck, protruding from underneath hollowed eyes. No longer able to look at his haunting reflection, he shuffled the mouse back and forth to awaken the screen. He opened a browser window and clicked away aimlessly in search of distraction. A Facebook friend request notification appeared at the top of the screen. He peered closer in order to read the small font – it was from Sally Fresco. Ryan's stomach flip-flopped as her profile picture appeared. 'Sally fucking Fresco' he muttered to himself, 'why the fuck would you friend request *me*?'

Sally had been Ryan's co-worker, and about two years ago, they had both applied for the same promotion. She had always been a thorn in Ryan's side, a real over-achiever. She had seemed so confident, charming and authoritative. Always the first in the office and the last to leave. She would go the extra mile, do that little bit more than was expected in order to 'wow' her clients. She had carefully honed her relationship with them, becoming an expert at anticipating their needs. The disappointment of failing to win the promotion had knocked her surprisingly fragile confidence, triggering a series of setbacks. She began to second guess herself. She made some bad calls. Her clients became nervous, requesting that their accounts be reassigned. This spooked the partners who responded by diverting new high worth clients away from her portfolio. It was a downward spiral that she was unable to stop, leading to her eventual management out of the business on the grounds of poor performance.

Ryan hadn't needed to work too hard in order to snatch the promotion for himself. Knowing that he was the only other candidate, all he had needed to do was to discredit Sally. And so while Sally Fresco tirelessly worked all hours, pulling out all the stops in order to impress the partners, Ryan did what Ryan did best. He sat back, did as little work as he could get away with and threw a colleague under the bus in order to get ahead. He'd started a rumour that Sally was pregnant and that she was withholding this information with the intention of going directly onto maternity leave once she had secured the promotion, and subsequent salary increase. The all-male team of partners panicked and immediately passed on her as their preferred candidate, giving the job to Ryan. He was pleased with himself at the time because it was a rumour that no one would ever try to verify with her for risk of being seen as either biased if she was indeed pregnant, or insensitive if she wasn't. But having subsequently watched her career spin slowly out of control, he had done his best to forget all about Sally. He hadn't meant things to go that far. Watching her unravel like that had been the beginning of Ryan's creeping realisation that maybe he was an asshole. The office had followed the fall of Sally Fresco with morbid fascination, a car crash happening in slow motion. The day that she was given her final marching orders was one that Ryan would never forget. She had left the board room looking shell-shocked, a vacant expression betrayed by a wildness in her eyes. The office fell silent as heads popped up above monitors like Prairie Dogs. She walked stoically to the lift and waited. Ryan didn't want to look, didn't want to face what he had done. But he couldn't help himself. Sally's bottom lip trembled as a tear rolled down her cheek. In an effort to hold herself together, she straightened her jacket while fussing anxiously with stray tendrils of hair. The lift finally arrived after an interminable wait. She stepped inside and turned to press the button, looking up and to see the eyes of the entire office upon her. It was too much. She lost control and dissolved into wild, desperate sobs. Everyone remained transfixed, starring in horror as the doors slowly closed on Sally Fresco. The office was silent until the lift reached the ground floor and the sound of Sally's crying could no longer be heard. Slowly, people began returning to their work and a low, awkward murmur replaced the uncomfortable silence. But Ryan was frozen, eyes fixed on the closed lift doors, the sound of Sally's sobs still ringing in his ears.

Ryan had done his best to push all of this from his mind. When that failed, he had tried to justify his actions; he had just done what was necessary in order to get the promotion. When that didn't help him sleep at night, he reasoned that he hadn't ever meant things to go that far; if he had known what would happen, he would never have started that rumour. And when none of that helped, he drank more, ate more, smoked more and slept less. He was locked in his own downward spiral, culminating in a massive heart attack and a diagnosis of heart failure. His condition was serious enough that he was placed on the transplant waiting list. A congenital defect had been exacerbated by poor diet, chain smoking, heavy drinking and severe stress. It had been the wakeup call that Ryan had needed. He had since retreated to his home office, too ashamed to show his face at work. He hid behind emails, phone calls and Zoom meetings. He had stopped the drinking and the smoking and had started to eat better. He set up a home gym and exercised daily. Over the period of a year he had shed five stone. He had also worked on his mental health. The experience with Sally and his subsequent heart attack had given him an epiphany; he was a terrible human being, living a terrible life. Sure, he'd not been given the best start by his parents, but he couldn't make them responsible for what he had done. And it wasn't just Sally. Below her was a whole career built on a foundation of similar casualties. Dozens of people that Ryan had stepped on and clambered across in order to get ahead. No, Sally was just the straw that broke the camel's back. But deep inside he seriously doubted that there was enough time to ever make up for what he had done.

How could he possibly put right what had happened to Sally? And what about the others? Now that his eyes had been opened, he couldn't close them. It was almost more than he could take.

Reluctantly, he accepted Sally's friend request and checked out her 'about' information. Did he know that she had kids? He was pretty sure that he hadn't cared. She belonged to several single parent support groups, was involved with a mental health charity, and took part in a monthly litter pick at her local park. Her news feed was a series of light-hearted complaints about the trials and tribulations of raising teenage twins with a useless, absent husband and father. There were photos of them together, Sally and the kids. Birthdays, trips to the beach, messing about at home. The usual sort of stuff, but they looked happy. She looked happy. The fact that Sally was raising two kids alone and had found a way to be happy, despite what Ryan had done to her, just amplified his guilt. He returned to the top of her news feed and read her most recent post. A photo of her beaten up old car, looking like a poster child for the scrap heap. The post went on to say that the car had failed it's MOT and was going to cost thousands to fix. She had no money to repair it and without it she had no way of getting her kids from A to B or get to work. She was fucked. Her words.

Ryan felt an idea forming. Could he do this? Should he? How would he? He was excited to have something to think about other than himself. Excited that there may be a way that he could do something to help Sally. And maybe atone for his guilt.

He opened a new browser window and started to research how he could anonymously gift a car. He found an online car sales company where you could buy a car completely online, and have it delivered. Ryan was giddy with excitement. He hadn't felt like this for….well, he hadn't ever felt like this. It was completely exhilarating. And just like that, he had bought Sally a brand new, family sized BMW. Ryan was aware that he couldn't just buy his way out of this. There was no amount of money that would undo the things that he had done. But it wasn't about the money. It was the gesture. The anonymous gesture and the impact that it would have on Sally's life. He almost giggled to himself as he imagined Sally's reaction. He sat back in his chair and felt just a fraction of the crushing weight that he had been living under, gently lift.

***

Sally poured cereal into two bowls, making a mental note that they needed more milk. She shouted up to the twins and poured herself a large coffee. She took a tentative sip, establishing that it wasn't too hot before taking two large gulps. The caffeine buzzed her and she felt a little more like she could face the day. She took another gulp and topped up the chipped 'Best Mum' mug.

"Come on!" she shouted louder, "Aunty Michelle is going to be here in ten minutes to drop you at school and me at work." She shoved a cereal bar in her bag for later and prepared the kids lunch boxes. She was just about to shout up to them again when there was a knock at the door. 'Fuck me' she exclaimed.

"Downstairs – NOW! She's EARLY!". She marched down the hall to get the door. Pulling it open, she was surprised to see a tall man in a smart suit standing in the doorway.

"Oh", she sighed. "Sorry, I was expecting someone else".

"That's ok…..Miss Fresco, is it?" the man looked down at his iPad and then back at Sally to confirm.

"Yes, that's me" she replied, an edge of impatience in her voice.

"Ok then Miss Fresco, I'm James from 'Cars to You.com' and I'm delivering your new car today" he said, in a bright, cheerful voice. He signalled behind him to the gleaming white BMW Tourer that was parked on Sally's driveway.

Sally was confused, caught off guard. "Sorry, James, I haven't ordered a car. I can barely afford milk. I think there's been an admin error somewhere"'

The peppy smile on James' face faltered a little, a wrinkle forming on his brow. He swiped quickly on his iPad, checking the details of the order. "Ah!" he exclaimed, the peppy smile returning. "I see what's happened. You're quite right, you didn't make the order. Someone else did, on your behalf."

Sally was irritated now. She didn't have time for this.

"I'm sorry – *what*? What do you mean someone has ordered a car, *on my behalf?* I'm not paying for that; I *can't* pay for that!" The twins heard the exchange and rushed down the stairs to see what was happening.

"Sorry Miss Fresco, I'm not explaining this very well. Someone, who wishes to remain anonymous, has ordered and paid in full for this car. It won't cost you a penny. I have all the relevant documents in this wallet. All you need to do is sign to take delivery."

"Holy crap, Mum! Do we have a new *car*? Is this *ours*?! It's *so* cool!" exclaimed the twins as they rushed past her and James. "Hey Mum, it's only a bloody M-Series!"

"Ben, watch your mouth! And don't touch anything, we're not keeping it." With that Ben pulled open the passenger door and William pushed him out of the way to get inside the car first.

"Miss Fresco, I assure you, this isn't a scheme or a scam. This is quite genuine. Google us if it would make you feel more comfortable".

Sally pulled out her phone and checked the website. She then checked 'TrustPilot.com' for any user reviews that suggested scamming or fraud. "I don't understand who would do this, it doesn't make sense. It seems too good to be true."

James tried to reassure her. "Miss Fresco, can I call you Sally?" When her reply was a blank stare, he coughed awkwardly and continued. "Miss Fresco, 'Cars To You.com' is a very large, reputable car sales business specialising in web ordering and home delivery. An anonymous client has ordered and paid in full for this car which is now registered in your name and is sat on your drive. It is legally yours and no-one can take it away from you. You just have to sign." He handed the iPad to Sally with a stylus. Still bewildered, she took them from James and read through the document. Knowing her way around a contract, she expertly scanned the wording for anything that was legally obtuse.

"Mum, MUM! It has heated leather seats! And TV's in the headrests!"

Sally ignored them while she did her due diligence on the document. It was true, there was nothing that could come back to bind her to a contract or a payment. It was clean.

"Why would someone do this? For me. Can you tell me who your client is?"
"Sorry Miss Fresco, the data protection act prevents me from doing that."

Sally thought about it for a moment. In her experience, when things seemed too good to be true, they usually were. The past couple of years had been one set back after another and this sudden windfall made her suspicious. Was life fucking with her? She didn't think she could cope with any more disappointment; she was a woman on the edge. But then she looked at the kids in the car. She hadn't seen them so excited in ages. Then she looked past the BMW to the heap of crap parked next to it – her existing car. And just like that, she made up her mind. "Fuck it", she said out loud. It was time to let go and embrace some good fortune, wherever or whomever it had come from. She signed her name with a flourish, taking the document wallet from James as she handed back the tablet and stylus. On impulse, she leapt forward and hugged him. Holding him for a little longer than was appropriate, she felt some of the tension inside her release, just a little. James was taken aback, and a little embarrassed. He thanked her awkwardly and shouted good-byes over his shoulder as he quickly walked down the driveway.

Sally called out to the twins. "Kids, get your stuff! Looks like I'm driving you to school!"

The twins were 'Christmas morning' excited as they bounced up and down in the back of the car and fussed over the controls for the TV mounted inside the headrests. Having barely pulled out of the drive, they had already synched Sally's iPhone to the CarPlay system. Cheerfully arguing over playlists, they pumped out the first five seconds of a song at ear splitting volume before changing it for another. Sally pretended to protest, but she was enjoying it. Seeing them so happy, being able to give this to them, filled her with joy. She watched them in the rear-view mirror as she gently squeezed the pedal, the BMW spiriting them down the street like a mobile nightclub. Sally marvelled at the acceleration, the comfort and sophistication of the car. LED screens flashed with various information pertaining to the cars performance, outside conditions and whatever the kids were doing in the back with the in-car entertainment system. After a short drive, she parked at the end of East Road, out of sight from the school where the twins had always insisted on being dropped off.

"Ok you two, out you get."
"No way Mum!' they laughed in unison. "You can drive us all the way to the school gate in this car!"

She knew that it was a shallow win, but Sally's heart swelled with pride anyway. She accelerated hard, the tyres screeching a little. The engine emitted a pleasing thrum as they pulled up quickly outside the school. The twins had turned up the volume of the music, causing the whole car to vibrate rhythmically. Sally caught the disapproving, but secretly covetous looks from the other school mums stood in clutches, arms tightly folded. She shot them a barely concealed 'fuck you' smile. The twins piled out of the car, the music spilling out with them. They made a big show of shouting their goodbyes and Sally obliged by tooting the horn and revving the engine as she pulled away.

She wondered at how the day was turning out so much better than it had started. She'd woken that morning with the usual lead weight in her stomach, the lurching butterflies of dread. How was she going to get through another day? How could she keep doing this, *every day?* It was overwhelming. But this morning had been a turning point. Good things *can* happen. There *are* good people out there, doing amazing things for others. It had restored her faith in humanity. Maybe the world wasn't always such a dark place. It was just at that moment that a young man wearing large headphones stepped off the curb, without looking.

***

Ryan was making breakfast when his phone rang. He pushed down the lever on the toaster and pulled the phone from his pocket. It was his consultant. He felt a rush of blood to his head as he fumbled with the phone to answer.

"Dr Walsh, good morning".
"Hello Ryan, how are you this morning?"
"Oh, I'm, um, I'm ok I guess. I didn't sleep very well actually but I'm up and about making some…"
"Good, good, nice to hear Ryan. So you need to come to the hospital as soon as you can. Now if possible. We have a donor."

Ryan froze, speechless.

"Ryan, I need you to focus. Time is of the essence."

"Yes, yes, I'm sorry. It's just, I wasn't expecting this. Not today, maybe not ever."

"Well, it's happening. Now. The heart is being transferred from the other side of London as we speak."

"That's amazing news Dr Walsh, really. I'm a little in shock. But I understand, I'll put a few things in order, pack a bag and be at the hospital within the hour."

"Very good Ryan, very good" and with that Dr Walsh ended the call.

Ryan stood motionless in his kitchen, phone still in hand, staring into space. Burning toast activated the smoke alarm, it's piercing squark bringing Ryan back to reality. 'Shit!' he muttered as he hastily removed the carbonised bread from the toaster. He quickly cleared the breakfast things away and made preparations for the hospital. His mind was racing, thoughts spinning. This was happening. There was a part of him that had come to terms with a reality where he may die young having lived a shallow, selfish and unfulfilled life. But he was being offered a second chance. Was this karmic payback for his good deed, he wondered? He thought about Sally. The last time that he had thrown a stone into the pond of her life, it had been a heavy, dirty and jagged rock causing dark ripples of ever decreasing circles. Maybe this time he had tossed a different kind of stone. A small, perfectly smooth pebble, triggering gentle ripples of positive change. Ryan considered this for a moment as he packed toiletries into a bag; it was the first time in his adult life that he had done something selfless, generous and kind without expecting anything in return. And yet it seemed that these ripples were extending outward in far reaching arcs, already finding their way back into his own pond.

8 The Velvet Shroud

A mischievous autumnal wind whistled along the street, kicking up dried leaves and sending them flying into the air where they danced enthusiastically in golden afternoon sun. Billy caught the comforting aromas of hearty, warming cooking emanating from the houses that he passed. Kids rushed by him on their way home from school, faces ruddy and cheery, keen to get inside to the warm. Billy removed his woolly hat, unzipped his heavy coat and unstuffed his hands from deep pockets. He wanted to 'feel' autumn. Feel the crisp air on his face, feel it whistling through the thin shirt fabric before finding his warm, bare skin beneath. He felt alive. It was invigorating. He took in a mindfully deep breath of autumnal air and held it in his lungs for a moment, visualising the oxygen as it surged through his body.

He exhaled loudly and resumed the walk to his local supermarket, mentally reciting the shopping list that he had prepared, and subsequently left on the kitchen table. Milk, bread, cat food (look for a new brand as Alexis III had grown tired of the current offering), something for his dinner tonight, loo roll, coffee, cat litter (look for a new brand as Alexis III no longer liked 'the feel' of the current brand on her paws), dishwasher tablets and stain remover (to remove the mark from his expensive bed linen; a memorandum in regurgitated form left by Alexis III in disdain of her current brand of cat food). Billy was sure that he had forgotten something from the list and was running through it again when he suddenly became aware of a presence, something in his personal space. Instinctively he turned his head, expecting to see someone at his shoulder. But there was no one there. He could hear whispering too, close by as if someone was leaning into his ear. He could even feel warm breath, could smell its unpleasant odour. He spun around as a shot of adrenalin was released into his system. An uneasy feeling crept slowly across his skin causing it to goose-bump. He continued walking, albeit it with some trepidation. He made an amendment to his mental shopping list; he would look for a decaffeinated brand of coffee. As he walked, he became aware of something in his peripheral vision. A glimmer. Something that was there, but not quite……there. Instinctively, he slowed his pace and turned his head.

Slowing to a stop, he stared across the street. There was that feeling again, that presence. And the sound, that whispering. 'What the fuck *is* that??', he thought to himself. Without consciously thinking about it, he found himself stepping into the street. A white van screeched to a halt as an angry woman leaned out of the window, shouting something colourful and obscene. He heard it, but somewhere at the edge of his consciousness, like hearing your name called out while you are deep in a dream. Without breaking his stride Billy continued to the other side of the street, trancelike and compelled by whatever was making that sound. He found himself walking down the side of Madam Rosina's Spiritual Emporium and into an access alley, littered with commercial bins and dumpsters. Tall buildings either side blocked out the autumn sun. It was cold, dark and dank. Cooing pigeons fussed around the bins, busy and hopeful in their search for food.

Reaching the end of the alley and not having located the source of the sound, Billy turned and found himself stood before a full-length mirror shrouded in worn, red velvet. A tear in the fabric revealed a section of chipped, gilded frame and cracked, smoky glass.

    Billy stood before it, unable to move. Unwilling to move. He took another deep breath and exhaled, his body becoming soft and limp. His shoulders dropped as a lifetime of tension, stress and worry were spontaneously released. He let out an involuntary sigh as he resigned himself to something that he couldn't comprehend. Time passed; the lazy autumn sun gave way to a bright, luminous moon. Stars pinpricked the sky and the air turned cold, frosty. Pigeons took shelter in a nearby abandoned garage and the alley fell silent. Silent aside from the sound of Billy's breath, sending out soft, billowy white clouds into the cold night air. And silent aside from that whispering, maddeningly on the cusp of being intelligible. Billy strained his ears. It was soft, soporific and hypnotic. It seemed to be coming from the mirror, but at the same time, from much further away. He leaned forward and turned his ear to the mirror, his hair brushing against the velvet.

"mrdhfudhfurremovehhbhhjvfvbfthehfdihhshro udjhhjfbvjfyouhbdbcjdfbwantjhdfjbjsfctojbdfjbfremove njfdkvhkjfdthejfhdkhvshroud".

Billy thought that he could discern words in amongst the ramblings, hiding like a code. He pressed his ear hard against the fabric now, feeling the cold glass beneath. Suddenly he heard it. A small, pleading voice, brittle like the frosty night air.

"Remove the shroud, you want to remove the shroud".

For a moment, Billy was ripped from his trance as he jumped back from the mirror in shock. Shivers ran up and down his spine as the fine hairs on his arms stood on end. Suddenly, he was aware that day had turned to night. That he was cold and hungry. He heard music spilling into the alley from a nearby pub as a fire escape door opened and closed again. The soft, soporific murmurings resumed. Billy was once again entranced, eyes drawn to the shrouded mirror. He noticed for the first time that there were symbols stitched into the fabric. Moons, stars and hexes in fine, silver thread. Gently tracing them with his index finger, he was strangely thrilled by the feel of the plush velvet. Following what he imagined to be a constellation, he worked his way up the tear, gingerly fingering the frayed edges. He allowed the tip of his finger to lightly touch the glass, as if it was in some way forbidden, taboo. He stroked it gently, playing with the cracked edge almost seductively before hooking his finger behind the shroud and tugging gently. It was weighty, snagging on the rough corners of the frame. Billy circled his remaining fingers around the fabric, clenched them into a fist before yanking it away from the mirror with sudden impatience. All at once he saw his reflection in the dark, smoky glass of the mirror. The image was distorted, disturbingly surreal in the cracked glass. He felt dizzy suddenly, losing his balance and falling forward. His heart skipped a beat as if he had been running down a set of stairs and missed the bottom step. Instinctively he covered his face but instead of smashing into the mirror, he stumbled forward into thin air. He paused for a moment, tensed, before uncovering his face and looking up. He was confused, disorientated. Before him was a graduated darkness, shades of grey disappearing into an inky black horizon. He spun around in panic. He could see the alley before him, but the mirror was gone. He spun around again to see the same dark void stretching out behind him. Turning his back on it again, he rushed forward to search for the mirror and smashed his face into something hard and cold. Stunned, he staggered backwards. Putting his hands out before him, he could feel an invisible wall. No, not a wall, and not invisible. It was glass. He was standing behind glass. He stepped back farther. Unfathomable darkness extended in all directions around this single rectangle of light, this window to the alley. Billy started to panic, a sense of terrible dread rising through his body. He beat his fists on the glass angrily, shouting, yelling for help. It was then that a figure appeared on the other side of the glass. Billy froze mid scream, his beating fists held motionless above his head as the colour drained from his face. A warm trickle of urine passed down the left leg of his jeans as his arms dropped, hanging limply at his side. Before him stood……stood himself. Moving closer to the mirror, it looked directly at Billy, studying him. It signalled for Billy to move closer. Stepping forward, Billy was terrified but unable to do anything else. He could see their breath, condensation on both sides of the glass. It looked directly into Billy's eyes, as if searching for something. It gave him the slyest, most sinister wink that Billy had ever seen, made all the more horrifying because it was coming from his own face. A broad, disturbing smile stretched across its mouth as it bent down to the ground.

"No, no, NO! Don't, please don't do that! Please, WAIT!" Billy shouted, pleaded, as it picked up the velvet shroud and draped it over the mirror before walking away from Billy and into the night.

9 Letting Go

I realise that I am standing still, that I have zoned out. I don't know how long I have been stood here like this. I can't even remember how I got here. I feel lightheaded, like my head is full of helium and I might just float away. I try to ground myself, but everything is strange, surreal. I try to focus and realise that I can't remember where I parked the car. I hit the remote unlock button. I see my lights flash somewhere over to the right and I start walking towards them in a trance. My legs are heavy, the air feels close and dense. Putting one foot in front of the other takes more effort than it should, as if I am wading through a river. My brain pushes painfully against the inside of my skull, as if trying to expand in order to process the unfathomable. A pressure is building, and I feel like an overinflated balloon, stretched too thin and about to pop. I find it hard to catch my breath as I become aware of a rising sense of panic. My skin starts to tingle, a dreadful creeping sensation travels up my spine and spreads across my scalp. Suddenly, getting inside to the relative safety of my car becomes the most important thing in my life. With a rising sense of panic, I urgently fumble with the door handle and maddeningly, drop the keys. It takes a monumental effort not to burst into tears. I retrieve them, pull open the heavy door and clumsily drop myself into the seat. I yank the door shut on the outside world, and as it closes with a satisfying thud I am instantly calmed by the hushed interior of the car and the reassuringly familiar smell of leather. The air is cool. I take the deepest breath that I can, hold it for as long as I can, and let it out all at once. I do this several times. And then I scream. A spontaneous, primal, throat burning, purge of a scream. It is so loud in this confined space, but that makes it all the more satisfying. My ears ring. I do it again. Louder this time and harder. I carry it on for as long as I can, gripping the steering wheel for dear life until the last puff of breath has left my lungs, and the scream tapers to a strangled whisper. I pause in that mysterious place between breaths before gasping a painful, urgent gulp of air. My throat is soar and my lungs are burning, but I feel something else too. The hot, sharp, urgent panic is now purged, giving way to an airy sense of calm, resignation and quiet certainty. You see, my entire life I have lived beneath a dark, menacing cloud. It follows me everywhere, threatening to rain down doom on me and those that I love, foreboding and throwing shade on any happiness that I might have, a constant warning that it can be wiped out with a tempest of abandonment, chaos and destruction. But what I have heard today, the diagnosis that I have just received, has dispersed it. Literally stealing its thunder and vaporising the stormy, brooding mass with an atomic explosion. And weirdly, perversely, all that remains is a vast, uninterrupted blue sky. For the first time in my life, I am free of that fucking cloud and its worst case scenarios, its 'what ifs'. And it feels incredible.

We always think that death is the worst thing that can happen to us, but living and enduring is so much harder. It's something that my dark cloud has taught me well; of all the things that I've worried about, dying has rarely been one of them. It is what I might have to live through that keeps me awake at night. What I might have to endure and survive. It is why I have always maintained an air gap between myself and anything or anyone good in my life, because having it and losing it would be far worse than never having had it at all. But that is over now. It seems suddenly so ridiculous to me.

I am all at once free of the fear of growing old and lonely, of living through the death of everyone that I have loved. Free of the fear of living in a world where not a single person can share a memory of my childhood, my family, my life. Free of the fear that I would be the last man standing in the short production that had been my life, remaining behind only to pull closed the red velvet curtains, all the other actors having long since exited left. I have spent so much time agonising over this scenario. It hangs over me like a weight, tempering my enjoyment of day-to-day life. But now? I can say with almost absolute certainty that I am never going to have to live through this.

And my fear of nuclear war, natural disaster or meteor strike and the subsequent breakdown of civilisation. How could I watch those that I love struggle for their very existence? As food supplies dry up and camaraderie gives way to primal instinct, could I savagely fight with my bare hands in order to secure food? And as we all begin to starve, as social order unravels, what would become of my dogs? Unable to feed even myself, what would happen to them? How could I endure that? How could I do what was necessary? But now, I can let it go. It's never going to happen. Well, it's unlikely to in the next three to six months, anyway. I haven't heard anything in the news about a wayward asteroid. And I check. Regularly. No leader of a nuclear nation appears to have a twitchy finger hovering above a large, red button at this point in time. I will live out what is left of my life, safe in the knowledge that it's not something I might have to live through. Again, it feels incredible that something that has given me nightmares all my life has now, suddenly, just gone. It's like receiving a cure for a terminal disease. Irony is a bitch.

My mind races, gleefully letting go of every fearful version of the future that I have been holding on to. Every worst-case scenario, each 'what if'. I am almost giddy with relief. I feel totally liberated, free from this crippling anxiety. It is exhilarating. I make a vow to myself; I say it out loud. I will live each minute of each hour of each day of each week of however many months that I have left. I will fully 'live' them. Totally present, totally mindful, all the time. I will live for the moments I have already squandered; live for the moments that I now won't see. I will condense them all down, live them fast and live them hard. I am not scared of dying, but living has always terrified me. Not anymore.

10 Out Of This World

The house was quiet. The TV that Donna kept on in the background had timed out and turned itself off. The absence of noise was profound, becoming a sound almost in itself. It was deafening. It pierced the muted oblivion where Donna had been hiding and she woke with a start, throwing off her blanket and causing Pilchard the border terrier to complete two full body rolls before coming to a stop at the end of the sofa. He let out a resigned sigh, before settling back down to sleep with a groan. Donna quickly got up and shuffled across the room. She clicked on the TV as she passed and called out to Alexa to read her the news. Throwing open curtains with a flourish, she headed for the kitchen where she turned on all the lights and fired up the coffee machine. Preheating the oven, Donna tried to hum a cheerful tune. It sounded macabre and surreal, at odds with how she felt inside, but she did it anyway. 'Fake it until you make it' was the latest, questionable advice from her expensive grief counsellor. Dark thoughts began to gather at the corners of her mind. She forced her mouth into a wide smile in an effort to release depression busting endorphins. Another piece of tinpot advice. She headed quickly to the front door to check the post, hoping for distraction. She busied herself in the same routine every morning, tip toeing around the sleeping Ogre that personified her debilitating anxiety. Donna had trained him over time to be a fairly heavy sleeper, and she had learnt that maintaining bright and breezy thoughts was the best way to avoid waking him.

She shuffled through the post. Junk mail, council tax bill, junk mail, exclusive broadband offer from Sky (junk mail) …. and then she saw it. Her humming trailed off, the forced smile fading, and her shoulders dropped. She felt winded. The walls began to close in as the ground beneath her feet shifted. She dropped the letter to the floor quickly, as if it were scolding hot. Seeing his name in print brought it all flooding back. The mere existence of the letter seemed to wrench him back from memory into reality, as if he could walk through the front door at any moment. It had taken time, but she had accepted now that he wouldn't. He was gone. But she had no idea where, why or how, and that is what had almost driven her mad. He had just vanished, literally. He'd left for work one morning and had never come back. All she could ascertain was that he'd arrived at the science institute, and that he'd had coffee with colleagues before locking himself away in his private lab. That was the last anyone had seen of him.

His work had always been top secret and he'd never dropped her even the faintest hint about what it was that he was working on. In the days before he disappeared, he'd become distant, completely absorbed by his work, almost fanatically. It was a familiar pattern when he was working on something new. He'd disappear down a rabbit hole, and she wouldn't see him for days. He'd work longer and longer hours and some days, into the night, falling asleep at the lab. And so when he didn't come home from work that night, she hadn't questioned it. When he didn't reply to her text in the morning, she had been pissed, but not worried. But when he didn't come home the next evening, she had started calling around.

And when it transpired that he hadn't been seen at the institute that day, that's when she had started to panic. That's when the wheels of her life had started to come off, and things had started to spin out of control. For the longest time, she had been suspended in a tortuous limbo. Had he run away? Had he left her? Was there another woman? Or maybe he'd been kidnapped for something that he'd been working on? Maybe something had gone terribly wrong at work. An accident in the laboratory perhaps, his death part of a government coverup conspiracy. She had cycled through confusion, anger, sadness, bewilderment and back to anger again before eventually settling on tenuous acceptance. With the help of her counsellor, a lot of wine and a cocktail of pharmaceuticals, she had levelled out to some sort of normality. But it was fragile, glass-like. She had such a shaky grip on her sanity that it often felt as if these morning rituals were all that stood between her and madness.

She stared at the letter on the doormat. She remained lost for a moment, trance like before her whispering thoughts as they enticed her into their dark fold. The clatter of her brooding ruminations had caused the Ogre to stir. He snorted and grunted as he turned over, dangerously shifting out of deep sleep into a lighter, more threatening level of consciousness. Donna nervously resumed the humming, louder now and with added vigour. Bracing herself, she gingerly pinched the letter between thumb and forefinger and marched it to the kitchen at arm's length. She gleefully fed it to her pet shredding machine that lived on the kitchen worktop. She had grown strangely fond of this hungry little gadget and its insatiable appetite for the toxic bombs that continued to drop through her letterbox. "There, there Brian, don't eat so fast – you'll give yourself indigestion" she cooed, patting his yellowing plastic as they banished the offending item from existence.

Donna put a frozen croissant in the oven and sat at the kitchen counter with a steaming cup of coffee while she distracted herself with her phone. It was the part of her morning ritual she enjoyed most; catching up with social media while sipping strong coffee and waiting for the caffeine buzz to lift her. As she switched from Facebook to Instagram, she tried to focus on a video of a canary taking a ride on the back of a cat. It was then that she became aware of a slow, flickering light in her peripheral vision. She looked up briefly, dismissing it as a reflection coming in through the kitchen window. But then the flickering sped up and increased in brightness, and was now accompanied by a low hum, a vibration. Donna could feel it through her chair, through her arm resting on the kitchen counter. She put down her phone and got off the stool. Something was reflecting on the back wall. It was a large rectangle, its edges clean and defined, while inside it was dappled and grey. She looked behind her for its source, but there was none that she could see. The humming intensified, becoming louder as the reflection started to gain more definition. As the flickering quickened to strobe-like speed, Donna squinted and shielded her eyes. The grey patches consolidated and darkened into a solid black mass, while lighter patches became smaller, but brighter and more intense. There was a sudden change in air pressure, and Donna's ears popped painfully. All at once, a surge of energy pulsed outwards towards her before snapping back to the wall with a loud cracking sound.

"What the fucking hell!" shrieked Donna as she stumbled backwards. The flickering stopped all at once, as did the vibration. Tentatively, Donna removed her hands from in front of her eyes and jumped back with a start. "Fucking hell!" she said again, and not knowing what else to do or say, "Fucking hell, fucking hell, *fucking hell!*"

Partly curious but mostly terrified, Donna stepped closer. She carefully reached out with her hand but snapped it back quickly when it passed straight through the wall. This wasn't a reflection at all. It was an opening. Donna stood inches before a large, door-sized opening into……into space? There was no other way to describe it. An inky black vacuum extended unfathomably into the distance, littered with billions of tiny, impossibly bright stars. She stood at the edge of it, feeling dizzy and confused. She was suddenly aware of Pilchard barking at her side, instinctively sensing danger. She absentmindedly reassured him, patting his head and sending him back to his bed, but he wouldn't leave her side.

Donna was caught in the middle of a fight or flight reflex, unsure of which instinct to follow. She probably would have chosen flight had it not been for a curious, bright circle of blue light that appeared somewhere in the distance. Then there was another, the same but larger and a little closer. And another and another, each one larger and closer than the last, forming a hypnotic tunnel effect. Donna quickly realised that whatever this was, it was moving towards her. Before she knew what was happening, she found herself stood before a wide, circular opening to a long tunnel of concentric blue circles, disappearing into the distance. She opened her mouth to say something, but no words came out. Until that is, her husband appeared at the opening of the tunnel. Donna closed her mouth. Then opened it again.

"Troy?" was all she could manage. There was so much to say, but it was all that she could verbalise. Pilchard began spinning around on the spot, excitedly.

"Oh Donna, you don't know how relieved I am to see you! I didn't know for sure that this would work. But there you are! And here I am! It's incredible! Light years apart, but also right here! How do I look? You're a bit blurry around the edges, maybe if I just..." he looked down at something Donna couldn't see and started to adjust it with a tool. Suddenly, Donna found her words.

"For fuck's sake Troy, after all these months and everything you've put me through, your biggest concern is that I'm a bit *'blurry around the edges'*?! I'll give you blurry around the fucking edges!" Donna wasn't even sure that this was real, she hadn't had time to process any of it. But she had been angry for so many months with nowhere to direct it, and right now, Troy, or a hallucinogenic version of Troy, was stood right before her and she needed to vent. "Where the fuck have you *been!* I thought I'd lost you! It's been nine months Troy! With nothing, not a single fucking word of explanation. You just leave me to go quietly out of my mind and then appear in the kitchen wall one Tuesday morning and all you can say is that I look *blurry?!*" Donna turned away from Troy in anger, and in a sudden moment of clarity, she had the presence of mind to turn off the oven before the acrid smell of her burnt croissant set off the smoke alarm. "And now I've burnt my fucking croissant. Thank you very much!" she screamed, as she threw it and the baking tray across the kitchen, sending Pilchard scurrying off back to the lounge. Donna broke down into sobs as she turned to Troy. "I don't understand. This can't be real, this doesn't make any sense, you can't be real, not here in the wall. I'm scared, I think I'm losing my mind" she blubbed as she slumped to her knees.

Troy put down the tool, knelt and held out his hand towards Donna. "I'm so sorry Donna, I really am. Not just for this, but for everything. All the times I've neglected you. There is nothing I want more than to spend the rest of my life saying sorry to you, and I will, but we really don't have time for that now. I will explain everything, but later".

"Later?", sniffled Donna.

"Yes, later, when you are here."

"What do you mean when I am *'here'*. Where is *'here'*? Where are you? How did you get there? Why are you coming to me like this? Why couldn't you just call me? I'm going to need a bit more than that as an explanation, Troy."

"Donna……..", Troy rubbed his head in frustration as he tried to think how to explain this all to Donna quickly, but in a way that wouldn't send her running for the hills. "I was working on something at the lab. An experiment. I stumbled across something, a way of travelling vast distances by manipulating time. It went too far; *I* went too far. I should have stopped, but I couldn't, I had to know. There was an accident and now I'm here, in a sort of……well, a sort of parallel universe for want of a better word. I can't get back to you, not yet. Maybe not ever. But I can use the same technology to bring you here. I've created this one-way time tunnel, but it will only hold for a short while Donna. You must decide".

"A parallel universe?" she said incredulously. "That's so typical of you Troy. Never thinking of how this might have affected me. And now you expect me to drop everything and just zap over there to be with you! My life is here Troy. And Pilchard – what about poor Pilchy! I couldn't leave him here all alone".

"He'd come too Donna! I think we could be happy here. It's like Earth but society has evolved at an exponential rate and enjoys an almost utopian existence. There's no war, no poverty, no climate change, no one ages or gets ill, and the broadband speeds are insane. How else do you think I'm managing what is effectively a FaceTime call from halfway across the universe!" Donna snorted a brief laugh, despite herself. It was classic Troy to make a joke at a time like this.

"I don't know Troy; this is too much to take in. Is it safe, you know, crossing over? Will I ever get to come back home?"

"Yes, it's almost completely safe Donna. And as for coming back, I honestly don't know. But we'd be together. That's all that matters to me. I don't care where that is. I just want to be with you. And Pilchard."

Donna didn't like the sound of *'almost'*, but Troy's *'almost'* was better than just about everyone else's *'completely'*, where science was concerned. She looked around her kitchen, at her sad cup of coffee and her burnt croissant. She looked at Barrie sat on the worktop and remembered how miserable she had been these past nine months. She struggled to imagine how long she could carry on like this. But still, what Troy was asking her to do. Her family, her friends. Her work. Her home, her life.

"Donna……." She turned back to Troy in horror as she saw his image flicker and fade. "Troy!" she yelled as he disappeared completely, and the tunnel started to retract into the distance. "Noooooooooo!" she sobbed as she got as close the wall as she could without falling through. "Troy, please come back, I'm sorry! I want to come, I just want to be with you too, I'm sorry I hesitated, I can't stand the idea of living without you, it's too hard, I can't do it anymore Troy, I don't think I can carry on like this much longer, I can feel myself fading away a little more each day……….."

With that, the tunnel and Troy snapped back into view as if someone had smacked the side of an aging TV in an effort to get a clearer picture.

"Sorry Donna, I knocked one of the wires. I didn't mean to frighten you".

Donna laughed with relief. "You complete dick Troy, I thought I'd lost you again! Wait there, I'll be right back."

"Donna, hurry…." Troy started but she was already gone. Giddy with excitement, she ran around the house, pulling things off shelves and out of draws and stuffing them quickly into a bag. It was impossible. How was she supposed to choose what to take? What she might need, or want? In the end she looked at the bag of random photos, keepsakes and memorabilia and decided none of it really mattered. It was just stuff. She dropped it on the floor, turned off the TV and scooped up Pilchard in her arms. "Come on Pilchy, we're going on an adventure".

She walked quickly to the kitchen to see Troy waiting for her in the tunnel. "Ok, I have everything we need" she said, looking down at Pilchard and kissing him on the head as they walked through the kitchen wall and into Troy's open arms.

11 Amber, Jade & Ruby

Fiona closed her eyes, took a deep breath and held it loosely for a moment. Jewel encrusted fingers stroked the quartz pendant that hung around her neck. She tried to clear her mind, tried to remember. Dappled sunlight danced playfully with her auburn hair, giving it a magical lustre as she sat cross legged beneath her tree.

Tilting her head gently towards the sky, she placed her palms onto the ground either side of her. She felt the warm, dry earth between her fingers as she grounded herself. Another deep breath, held for a few seconds longer this time before exhaling slowly, mindfully. She cast her mind back to July 7th, 1977. It had been a hot, stifling day. Fiona had been exploring the woods under the protection of its shady canopy. A half-hearted breeze found her legs, her arms, her neck, reluctantly cooling her with a listless sigh. She remembered wearing a light cotton dress, orange with a white and yellow daisy print. Her mother had insisted on a wide, floppy straw hat as ginger hair and a fair complexion meant that she would burn easily. She'd been fascinated by the bright sparks of dappled light that danced on the ground where she sat as the sun streamed through the small gaps in its brim. Much like the dappled light coming through the trees today, she realised, as a thrill of excitement passed through her. Is that a sign, she thought? Is it *auspicious*? Encouraged, she jiggled her position slightly, giving her pendant another rub as she focused her mind on that day in the woods.

Fiona had returned to this same spot on this same day for the past thirty-two years. Each time that she returned, she thought maybe this would be the year that they would appear to her again. She took comfort from this ritual, from recounting the story in her head, playing over the sequence of events as if she were watching her favourite movie. Initially, she had been naïve of the cruelty of others and their unwillingness to believe in something that they hadn't seen for themselves. She had been obsessed to the point that it was all that she could think about. But she was mocked and bullied mercilessly at school whenever she talked about her special friends in the forest. She had learned the hard way that this was something to keep to herself. And so, that is what she had done. Fiona stopped talking openly about that day. Eventually she would deny that it had happened at all, dismissing it as childhood fantasy. But she kept it alive in her mind, in her heart.

Nonetheless, over time the events of that day had taken on a myth-like quality to Fiona. What had once been vivid and real to her had slowly transitioned into something misty and fragile. In her darkest moments, she wondered if it had ever happened at all. A whimsical and imaginative child, had she unintentionally embellished, misremembered or just plain fabricated the story? Realising that she had allowed herself to become distracted, Fiona visualised releasing a bright red helium balloon, as she gently let the thought go. Sat perfectly still, she tentatively opened one eye and scanned the area using only the movement of her eyeball. Like a sleepless child on

Christmas Eve, she tried to catch a glimpse of something that didn't want to be seen.

Fiona pulled out a wooden box from her canvas bag. It was decorated with fake plastic gems of amber, jade and ruby. Faded depictions of fairies carefully cut out from books and magazines as a child had been lovingly glued to its lid. She opened the box with great reverence as she regarded her treasured keepsakes. She fingered the fabric of the orange daisy print dress. She felt a release of endorphins as she made a physical connection to that ethereal day. Very carefully, she removed a small gauze pouch filled with brittle, dried flowers. She held it in her hand before her like an offering. With eyes closed, she wished as hard as she could. After a few minutes, Fiona began to feel silly and foolish. She carefully placed the gauze pouch back into the wooden box for another year and closed the lid gently. She held it to her chest and thought that she might cry.

She had never been able to recreate what had happened that day. She had no other evidence to suggest that it was anything other than a childhood daydream, evolved into personal folklore from repeated telling. But she just couldn't let it go. She wouldn't give up on those translucent, barely-there trio of fairies in crystal gem shades of amber, jade and ruby that had appeared to her on that magical day. She had played with them for a precious few minutes as they danced like butterflies around her, tugging playfully at her long curly hair and letting out giggles that sounded like tiny panes of the thinnest glass, gently shattering. They had made a necklace for her, working together in mid-air to thread wildflowers in an intricate pattern, right before her wide, wonderous eyes. They flew over her head as they lowered it gently around her neck. Fiona had put out her hand to touch the ruby coloured fairy, who'd at first backed away, looking alarmed. Eyes like tiny glass beads narrowed and regarded her suspiciously. Fiona had reassured her that she meant no harm; she just wanted to be friends. Her eyes softened as she giggled again. With a flutter of sparkling wings, she flew slowly to approach Fiona's outstretched hand.

But Fiona had strayed too far, had been gone too long. Her mother's loud voice boomed through the quiet woods. She reluctantly turned away from the fairies to call back to her mother, to tell her to come at once to see what she had found. But when she looked back to them, they were gone. She had searched around the tree anxiously, certain that they were teasing her, that they would appear from behind a patch of dandelions with that strange laughter of theirs. When platitudes and reassurances did not make them reappear, she had started to beg, and then to cry.

Her mother had pulled her away, admonishing her for straying so far. A practical and straightforward woman, she'd had little time for Fiona's tall tale of fairies. She had pleaded and cried as her mother led her by the hand back to the car.

Fiona's eyes began to moisten as she lamented the loss of the girl in the daisy print dress. She stood awkwardly, legs stiff from being sat cross-legged. Having smoothed the creases in her summer dress, she fussed with loose tendrils of hair. Taking one more hopeful look around the tree, she reluctantly turned her back on it and slowly walked away. Maybe next year, she consoled herself. But then Fiona was all at once arrested. She froze mid step, a tingling sensation at the back of her neck. Her whole body vibrated with impossible excitement. She had only heard that sound once before, but she would never forget it. The sound of tiny panes of the thinnest glass, gently shattering.

12 Annooska

Annooska exhaled, releasing the tension from her shoulders. Sat before a mountain vista, she lost herself in glacial waters, towering white peaks and an impossibly blue sky. Taking in a deep breath, she could smell the fresh, mountain air. There was so much space here, so much light. And it was so…. quiet. Annooska wanted to stay in this moment, forever. She was free here.

She settled her gaze on a bird of prey as it circled silently, high in the empty sky above her. She wondered for a moment how it would feel to be that bird. To be free, to live as nature had intended. Annooska was lost in her daydream when the scene freeze-framed, a message notification blotting the serene, blue sky and bringing her unwillingly back into reality. Irritated, she swiped it away with a dismissive flick of her index finger. After an initial judder, the bird resumed its flight and she tried to find her way back to the moment, but it was gone. With a larger gesture this time she dismissed the holographic display panel entirely and along with it, her moment of fantasy. She turned her thoughts to more practical matters; breakfast.

Unlike the bird of prey, hunting unnoticed in an empty sky for its sustenance, Annooska loaded the AutoChef 500 with programmable food matter and selected eggs Florentine, twice.

She called out to Treigh as she waited for her selection to finish printing. She drummed her fingers impatiently on the work surface, standing before the machine as it whirred and buzzed. Just as breakfast was ready, her wrist vibrated with an alert. She pulled out a hot tray of steaming eggs with one hand as she glanced at the watch on her free wrist. And then she froze, the heat from the tray working its way through the tea towel she was holding it with. All at once she registered that her hand was burning, and she instinctively dropped the tray to the floor.

Hearing the commotion, Treigh rushed into the kitchen. "Annie, what happened, are you ok?"

"I don't know, I..." she stuttered. "I..... I just burned myself and dropped breakfast. Can you clean it up while I sort out my hand?" Treigh activated the Robomaid and reprogrammed a fresh breakfast. Noticing its absence from the kitchen floor, he added bacon to the programme. Meanwhile, Annooska pulled the Medicaid from its dock on the wall and scanned her throbbing hand. Identifying a minor burn, it administered a healing programme, instantly relieving the pain. She pulled her personal device from her pocket and called up the notification. She read it, reread it and then read it again, but it wasn't sinking in.

"Annie, are you ok? What's that you're reading?" Treigh finished serving up breakfast and approached her from behind, putting a consolatory arm around her shoulder. Agitated, she shrugged it off. "Hey!" he said, defensively, "What's going on with you?" When she didn't respond or turn to face him, he moved to stand in front of her. She was staring blankly at the device, almost through it, all expression and colour drained from her face. "I'm pregnant" she whispered, the two almost inaudible words falling like tiny little bombs.

"No you're not", he blurted out. "That's impossible. Annie, you can't be, what are you talking about?" Treigh was confused.

"It's right here on my fucking wrist Treigh!" she shouted angrily, holding her wrist up for him to see. Annooska was confused too. And terrified. "This morning's bioscan picked up a change in my hormone levels and it says there's a 95% chance that I'm fucking *pregnant*!" Hot tears threatened in the corner of her eyes as she tried to fathom how this might have happened.

Treigh took a step back from Annooska as he ran a trembling hand through his long, black hair, still damp from the shower. This can't be right, he thought. This can't be happening.

The hot tears that Annooska had been holding back suddenly sprung from her eyes as she let out an involuntary sob. Brought back into the moment, Treigh caught her as she crumpled before him into a heap on the kitchen floor.

"Hey, hey, come on, come and sit down and we'll work this out. It's going to be ok" he said. There is no way that this is going to be ok, he thought to himself. He sat Annooska down at the kitchen table, clearing away the breakfast things and noticing that his appetite had completely vanished. He pulled out a chair from across the table and sat next to her, his arm around her quivering shoulders.

"I don't understand" he said as calmly as he could manage. "This shouldn't be possible, should it? We aren't unblocked, we haven't even applied! Do you think the test could be wrong?"

"I don't think so, these things are pretty accurate" she said, wiping away tears with the sleeve of her oversized jumper. "It says 95%. That's a pretty small margin of error Treigh!" she sniffed. "Do you think, I don't know, I know it's silly, but do you think it could be some kind of ….miracle?" She heard how ridiculous it sounded, but she continued. "I mean, you know how much we've talked about having a baby. How hard we've worked to build our support network, how hard you're working to get that promotion. How we've gone without so much in order to save what credits we can. Our entire lives have been about increasing our score. But just as we get a bit closer, they raise the bar a bit higher. You need so many points now, it's ridiculous. It's becoming a pipe dream for people like us to start a family. But then this happens. Maybe, I don't know, maybe it's………a sign?"

Treigh looked at her incredulously, but he spoke with caution, taking her hands into his as he leaned into her.

"Annie, if this test is right, if you really are pregnant, you know we can't keep it. I know it's what we want, I know it's everything we've been working for. But……well, we just can't. We haven't even applied to be unblocked. And even if we applied right now and tried to cover up the time discrepancy, there is no way that we'd be approved. We don't meet the financial criteria, I don't actually have that promotion yet, we have a questionable genetic profile with my mother's bipolar and your brother's diabetes, and we live in a tiny unit with no room for a baby".

Annie broke eye contact and settled her gaze at the kitchen floor, another hot tear rolling down her cheek.

"But maybe we could do this under the radar, maybe we could move out of the city where there are less people watching, less people to explain this to. We could go off-grid a little".

"Off-grid? A little?" Treigh said a little harshly, regretting his tone instantly. He was trying hard to hide his frustration, his fear. "Annie, this isn't a temporary problem. This is a lifelong problem. For us and for the baby. He or she won't be registered, won't be in the system. That means no healthcare, no school, no formal education. And even if we home school, the kid won't get an identification card and so will never be able to get a job. We'd be condemning him or her to a severely restricted life. Do you think that's fair? Don't you think he or she would resent us for that?" Annooska was about to protest, but he pressed on. "And that's just the child. What about you? You won't have access to any medical treatment during pregnancy. No midwife. We'd have to go it completely alone. That's so dangerous Annie. To you, to the baby, to *us*."

Annie started to say something, and then stopped. She paused for a moment, trying to come up with a counter argument, but she couldn't find one. As much as every fibre of her body was compelling her to protect this unborn baby, she also knew that Treigh wasn't wrong. Lost in the swirling vortex of her emotions, she almost missed the buzzing coming from her wrist.

"Oh fuck Treigh, oh fuck, oh fuck, oh FUCK!"

"What is it, Annie, what's wrong now?" When she didn't answer, he took the device gently from her. He read the notification and looked up at her carefully, as if she were a primed incendiary device.

"It's already too late Treigh, we're in the system. The test results have triggered an appointment with an OBGYN and an interview with the FPS. What are we going to do? Treigh? What are we going to fucking do?!"

Treigh's mind raced. This was bad. There was no hiding from this now. Annie's plan to run away and live off-grid might have been ludicrous, but at least their crime wouldn't have been known to the state. Now they'd be fucking fugitives.

"Maybe we should go along with this, just tell them that this is some kind of miracle, that we haven't done anything wrong. I mean, we haven't! What possible evidence could any investigation come up with that could incriminate us? We're completely innocent Treigh!"

Treigh snapped, his frustration at her naivety breaking through the thin veneer of his patience. "For fuck's sake Annooska, don't be so fucking naïve! They don't need fucking proof! The block is widely accepted as being 100% effective. If there's no record of a legitimate and legal unblocking procedure, they'll conclude that we've had it done illegally and they'll convict us. They won't need to look for fucking evidence! They'll terminate the pregnancy, drop a huge fine on us and we can kiss goodbye to ever getting a licence. Ever!" It was Treigh's turn to let his emotions overwhelm him now as angry tears sprung from tightly closed eyes as he held his head tightly in shaking hands.

Annooska was completely disarmed to see Treigh like this. He was usually so calm, so rational. Always steady, always sure. To see him unravel was heart breaking and it distracted herself from her own emotional turmoil long enough to get some clarity. She couldn't rely on Treigh to resolve this. It was too much to put on him. He loved her completely and she knew that if she insisted on keeping the baby, he would eventually relent and support her. Support them. Beyond the day-to-day squabbling and mundane arguments, Treigh would follow Annooska to the end of the earth and off the edge of a jagged cliff, if she asked him to. It was one of the things she loved about him, but also one of the things she sometimes resented; when it came to a crisis, she couldn't rely on him to take control when she needed him to. He would always ultimately defer to her judgment, putting a huge burden of responsibility onto her shoulders. She knew that if she asked him to, he would run away with her and that she'd ruin both of their lives in the process. Not to mention that of the unborn baby. Annooska leapfrogged from an unsurmountable problem to a pragmatic, logical solution in just a few moments, vaulting over all emotion and ethical argument because really, they were irrelevant. There was only one thing that they could do to save the three of them. And it broke her heart.

She spoke quietly, with a steady voice. She could hear the words coming out of her mouth, but they sounded disembodied.

"Then Treigh, I think we are only left with one option. I can't believe I'm saying it, but I think we need to consider finding somewhere that can take care of this." Something broke inside of Annooska as she put her fingers through Treigh's hair and reassured him that everything was going to be ok, that they would figure this out together. She was quite sure that everything was not going to be ok. The existence of the Fertility Planning System meant that there were no unplanned pregnancies, and therefore no legal abortion clinics.

They leaned into each other, gently bumping foreheads. She was comforted by the woody scent of his beard oil and his fresh, clean cologne. She was taken back to the mountain vista with its glacial waters, towering white peaks and impossible blue sky. She thought again of the circling bird.

They rested quietly like that for a while, listening to the sound of each other's breath and taking refuge in the eye of the storm.

Once more, there was a buzzing at Annooska's wrist. They pulled back from each other as she checked her device, blinking away drying tears. Reading the message, she dropped the device to the floor as if it were hot, just like the breakfast tray minutes before. A hot ball of grief, anger and relief formed in her gut. Her stomach cramped and she leapt up from her seat, sending it flying across the kitchen floor. Treigh quickly scooped up the device as he rushed over to Annooska and held her hair while she vomited into the sink.

***

<<< Saturday 4th June 8.23am – a self-diagnostic check on your device identified a biometric calibration error, which has now been rectified. The positive pregnancy notification received on Saturday 4th June at 7.53am was erroneous and should be ignored. A biometric test has since been rerun and a negative result returned. Please ignore all previous messages and notifications >>>

13 Creep Feeling

Brian added Coffee Mate to a chipped Christmas mug and stirred. Pulling back a mildewy net curtain, he peered through condensation at the street outside as he sipped the unpleasant brew. The whitener did its best to add some smoothness to the acrid, cheap coffee, but it was a lost cause.

'Why do I drink this shit?' he thought to himself, rolling his eyes at two teens in shirt sleeves as they roughhoused past his window on this cold, damp, December morning. He took another sip and winced. Not knowing that it was the last time that he would ever taste coffee, he poured the rest into the sink and vowed to order himself a Nespresso machine.

Brian glanced at the digital clock on the microwave. It was 07:45 and he was already restless. He stood for a moment, prone with indecision. He hated dead time. The entire day stretched out tortuously ahead of him, unstructured and interminable. The creeping sense of dread began to slither under his skin. Suddenly aware of a presence, a feeling that he was not alone in his kitchen, he turned around, expecting to see someone behind him. When there was no one there, he felt an urgent need to move, as if to dodge an imminent, but unseen threat. On impulse, he grabbed his coat and keys from the hook on the wall and promptly headed out of the front door. Walking quickly into the cold and gloomy morning, Brian couldn't shake the feeling that he was outrunning something. An uneasy feeling that he was being watched by an oppressive and malevolent force had plagued him for weeks, and it was starting to get to him. Sleep was illusive and his dreams were disturbed and surreal. He worried that his resulting tiredness was making him irrational and paranoid.

    A biting gust of wind cut through Brian's jacket and the jumper beneath it, chilling him to the bone. A notification buzzed from his inside pocket. Checking the message, Brian stepped off the curb to cross the street and into the path of a speeding Deliveroo cyclist, who shouted an angry warning in a language Brian didn't understand. The hand gesture that followed however, was universal. His heart skipping a beat, Brian quickly stepped back onto the pavement. The cyclist continued his tirade of exotic expletives, spitting at Brian as he passed. Outraged, Brian shouted after him. "Sorry mate, it was an honest mistake, but there's no need to be a fucking prick about it." The cyclist slowed to a stop before turning to stare at Brian aggressively. Instantly regretting his confrontational words, Brian's face fell, betraying his cowardice. Satisfied that Brian had quickly backed down, the cyclist gave a parting hand gesture and peddled off. Brian didn't know it, but those unprofound words would be his last.

Turning up the collar of his winter coat against the cold wind, he carefully crossed the street. He felt a sense of yearning as he noticed an advertisement on the back of a passing bus for Stanley, Cooper and Melrose, his firm. It was the first day of his leave and already he was counting the days until he could return. The internal politics, the power plays, the backstabbing and passive aggressive company speak; he hated it all.

The place was a relentless sweatshop for professionals, although lately he had become grateful of it; the unyielding workload sucked up virtually all of his time, providing distraction from this growing sense that he was being watched. But his boss had forced him to take annual leave after several colleagues raised concerns about Brian's increasingly odd and paranoid behaviour. The firm had experienced two workplace suicides in the past few years and had reacted by implementing a lip service mental health policy. They weren't interested in what was wrong with Brian, with what he might be going through, or in helping him to resolve it. But they wanted him off the premises while he sorted it out for himself. Or didn't.

Brian didn't know it, but he might as well have put all thoughts of Stanley, Cooper and Melrose out of his mind because he would never walk through their polished brass revolving doors again.

Realising that he had been walking without direction, Brian made a snap decision to head to Beyond Beans, his independent coffee shop of choice.

He enjoyed its funky, bohemian vibe, even if it was meticulously designed to look effortlessly accidental. He enjoyed even more the bearded barista with his flirty green eyes and tight shirt. Buoyed by a sense of purpose, he took a short cut through a back alley that ran behind the shopping centre. It was dark, with high buildings either side blocking out any hope of sunlight. The air was musty and damp with the unmistakable whiff of urine. As he stepped over a broken beer bottle and a half-eaten kebab, Brian suddenly became aware of a flickering light coming from somewhere above his head. As he looked up, the light became much brighter, dazzling him so that he was unable to see its source. He instinctively ducked his head and crouched down a little in a defensive action. He raised his hand to shield his face as the flickering light intensified further and began to strobe. Brian felt a change in the air somehow, an increase in pressure accompanied by a low hum that reverberated through his entire body. He closed his eyes as a wave of nauseating vertigo passed over him. He fell to where the floor should have been, but he didn't make contact with the dirty concrete. Instead, there was just an uneasy sense of weightlessness as air whooshed past him at high speed. He could feel pressure building at the top of his head as his ears popped painfully. Brian began to feel lightheaded and giddy and just as he thought that he might pass out, everything came to an abrupt stop.

Whooshing air was replaced with with an eerie stillness. Strobing lights with absolute dark. A crushing pressure on his chest replaced the sense of airy weightlessness. Brian was aware of being laid flat on what felt like a hard, cold slab of metal. As he instinctively tried to sit up, there was a terrifying realisation that he was unable to move. Confusion was quickly replaced with a rising sense of panic. The beginnings of a scream were held mid- breath in his chest when a razor thin shard of light pierced the darkness before him. Curious at first, unsure of what it was that he was looking at, Brian quickly returned to fear and panic as he felt intense heat and then burning, as the laser blade moved towards and then into his skull.

14 Barry & Barbra

Fussing with the plastic flower pinned in her hair gave Barbra a sense of comfort. She set the heavy pool bag down onto hot concrete and shielded her eyes from the sun. It was surreal, she thought, that one could be in two such different places within the very same day. She had woken at 4am that morning in her small mid-terrace house in Liverpool. She dressed quickly in clothes laid out the night before and despite the hour, enjoyed a simple breakfast of boiled egg and toast, sipping sweet tea from Barry's 'World's Best Grandad' mug. A car pulled up outside as she was clearing away the breakfast things. Turning off the kitchen light, she headed down the dark hallway to collect her case. Stood by the front door, her hand hovered over the latch as she hesitated for a moment. 'Am I really going to do this?' she thought to herself. Planning this trip had been an adventure. It had made her feel alive, brave and independent. She hadn't felt like that in a long time. It had also been a welcome distraction; time spent researching resorts, shopping for holiday paraphernalia, packing, unpacking, and then repacking was time that she hadn't spent thinking about her Barry.

The sound of the taxi driver's horn had brought her back into the moment. Before any further doubt could creep in, she took a deep breath and remembered the blunt, but wise words of her friend Sylvia when she had confessed to being scared to take the trip alone. "You're a long-time dead Barb…just ask your Barry." She struggled with her ancient burgundy case down the slippery footpath that cut through her neat little garden to where to the taxi was waiting. She had hoped that the driver might jump out to help her, but unwilling to move from his heated seat, he instead simply activated the remote boot release. Muttering mild exclamations under her breath, she somehow managed to wrestle the heavy case into the car. Doing things for herself was something that Barbra had been getting used to, recently.

But now she was here, in Gran Canaria! More specifically, the Beverley Park Resort. Eyes watering, she squinted into the sun and remembered the new sunglasses that her favourite grandson had picked out for her. She rummaged in her 'Pride' pool bag and produced the oversized pair of white rimmed sunglasses that had Declan said made her look like Jackie Kennedy. She'd laughed at her reflection in the mirror, saying that she looked more like Johnny Depp's Willy Wonka, than Jacki-O.

She knew that she shouldn't actually have favourites, and she loved all eleven of her grandchildren a great deal. But Declan was special, different from the others. He was a sensitive boy, and he'd had a hard time fitting in with the rough and tumble dynamic of their large, boisterous family. He would always seek out Barbra and confide in her about all manner of things. Barbra found some of it hard to listen to, not fully understanding his feelings or indeed, his generation. But she loved him unconditionally, independently from whom it was that he decided to love, and that to Barbra was really all there was to it;

he loved boys and not girls. Aside from that, he was just the same as anyone else. She hoped that one day he would feel that way too. But until he did, Barbra went out of her way to make Declan feel accepted, that he was fine just the way he was. She hid her shock or confusion at the some of the more colourful things that he would reveal to her about himself and his life. Even if she was reeling on the inside, she would nod acceptingly and offer some comforting words until she was alone and could look up what he had said to her on the internet.

Barbra took in her surroundings. It was just like she had imagined, and she was thrilled. She stood at the edge of a kink in the lazy river as it weaved its way through a clump of palm trees. To her left the river opened into a wide, shallow pool where mums and dads splashed about with excited children. She stood for a moment, feeling warmth on parts of her body that hadn't been exposed to direct sunlight in years. A gentle breeze carried the intoxicating scent of tanning lotion as the palm trees swayed listlessly. Barbra let out a deep breath, one that she had been holding in for a long time. She scanned the area for a suitable sun bed; somewhere tucked away a little, and with some shade. She cooled herself with a paper fan that she had bought from home, purchased another lifetime ago when she and Barry had holidayed in Torremolinos. It was decorated gaudily in a scene of technicolour bull fighters and flamenco dancers, edged in frilly black lace. The breeze picked up and caught her peacock print sarong as it billowed outwards and upwards like a resplendent multi-coloured sail. For a moment she was a reluctant work of art, framed in floating fabric as she held a languishing hand to her brow, searching for something unseen in the distance.

It was then that she noticed two handsome young men watching her. One was blond and pretty looking, the other dark and handsome. Both wore nothing, but the smallest, tightest speedos she had ever seen. They were leaning into each other, talking quietly behind cupped hands while looking directly at her. Barbra's heart sunk a little; were they talking about her? Or even laughing at her? Suddenly, she felt like a fool. 'What am I doing here, making a spectacle of myself in this getup', she thought to herself. Barbra's fragile self confidence faltered as she stopped fanning herself, her shoulders dropping a little. She instinctively clutched at the fabric of her sarong and tried to cover some of the exposed flesh in a subconscious effort to make herself less noticeable, smaller. She wished that the ground would swallow her up.

Matthew and Steve were in awe of the regal goddess that had appeared before them in an apparition of floating technicolour fabric. Matthew speculated that she was a famous actress from the days of the silver screen, a Hollywood siren who defied age and convention, blazing her own path of individuality. Steve favoured that she was a legendary fashion designer, a Parisian icon visiting Gran Canaria for a photo shoot. Matthew and Steve were enjoying their game when they noticed that her statuesque posture had become hunched, her enigmatic smile fading as her face crumpled. As her eyes met theirs, they realised at once that she thought they were mocking her, rather than admiring her. Quickly,

Matthew flashed her a disarming smile, held out his arm and wagged his index finger at her in camp drama, mouthing "F_A_B_U_L_O_U_S_!"

Instinctively, Barbra turned her head to see who the pretty blond man was pointing at. When she turned back and saw that he was still smiling at her from ear to ear, the penny dropped. She felt a swelling in her chest, a soaring of her spirits, a spark of something long forgotten. They were *admiring* her! Barbra felt like she had been plugged in to a high voltage outlet. Suddenly she was interesting and wonderful, not sad and ridiculous. She was reminded of her younger self, when she had been just Barbra and not one half of Barry and Barbra. She had been young then, beautiful and vivacious. By day she wore a disguise of tweed suits and pearls, working as a telephonist in a stuffy solicitor's office. But by night, she was transformed in homemade Mary Quant inspired creations, as she bussed drinks at a trendy cocktail bar in the city. She made a point of remembering the orders of her regulars and on seeing them arrive, she would dance over to them with their cocktails held aloft on a silver tray before they had even approached the bar. She would flirt, laugh at their jokes and remember details about their lives, but she would never allow them to touch her. She had a reputation for cutting customers down with a withering look and a sharp retort if ever they were foolish enough to cross the line; she was popular, but also respected. And she made a fortune in tips.

But then she met her Barry and quickly fell in love. Her night-time alter-ego was not compatible with being one half of Barry & Barbra and so she traded it all in for being a wife and a mother. And then a grandmother. She didn't complain, she was happy to make the compromise. She missed her old life from time to time, missed her old self, but Barry had been her soulmate and she'd loved him completely. Once the kids were grown, Barry and Barbra had moved into a new phase of their own lives, with time to pull back and rediscover each other. But then Barry had died unexpectedly, and she had been set adrift; being one half of Barry & Barbra no longer made sense.

And that is why she had planned this holiday, to somehow try and find herself again, as ridiculous as that sounded to her at the age of 78. But seeing herself through Matthew & Steve's eyes had awakened something in her. Giddy with excitement, Barbra selected a nearby sun bed under a swaying palm tree and unpacked some items from her pool bag onto the adjacent side table. A couple of racy paperbacks, sun block, an inflatable travel pillow and a clean beach towel from home (who knew how many grubby bodies had been dried with those supplied by the hotel?) Finally, she carefully lifted out a small, framed photo. Out of context, it looked surreal in the harsh Canarian sunlight. She felt both fondness and sadness as she planted a gentle kiss on the glass before placing her Barry onto the table beside her.

With all the grace that her mildly arthritic body would allow, she lowered herself onto the sun bed and caught the eye of a passing waiter, holding aloft a silver tray. She checked her watch and shrugged, an idea forming.

"Excuse me young man, but you'll make this old woman's day if you can answer 'yes' to the following two questions." She gave him a playful wink as she dusted off some of her cocktail waitress charm. The waiter raised an eyebrow and gave her a crooked, conspiratorial smile. She continued, "1- do you serve cocktails at this time of the day, and 2- do know how to make a mai tai?"

The waiter knelt one one knee next to Barbra and looked directly into her eyes, his own impossibly blue, like the Aegean Sea. "It is my life's pleasure to make the wishes of beautiful young ladies come true" he said, as he returned her a wink.

Long forgotten neural pathways were re-firing now, as Barbra revelled in the playful banter. She looked over to see Matthew and Steve slack-jawed and wide-eyed, both of them delighting in this delicious exchange. With confidence surging through her aging veins, she winked at them as she beckoned the waiter back to her.

"You see those two handsome young men just over there", she gestured behind the waiter. He looked over his shoulder and nodded, smiling. "Well, they look like a couple who appreciate a cocktail at 10 a.m. in the morning. Send them two of what I'm having please." The waiter laughed warmly, his eyes sparkling as he gently touched her arm in confirmation.

As he left, Barbra looked over to 'the boys' (that's how she'd refer to them when she befriended them later, she decided) and peered over the top of her sunglasses. Flashing them one of her long-forgotten trademark smiles, she held out her arm and wagged her index finger in camp drama at them both, mouthing "T_H_A_N_K_Y_O_U".

15 While The Kettle Boiled - Miss z

She turned to face the sea of hungry photographers one more time, a hundred or so cameras lifting to meet her gaze as she did so. It should have been a thrill. A cheap thrill, but a thrill none the less to command such attention. She decided to throw them a bone as she busted a move from her latest music video, sending the cameras into a frenzy. Thousands of photographs were taken in a matter of moments. Again, she should have felt electrified, exhilarated. She should have felt *something*. Each shutter release provided empty calories that would never satisfy her insatiable appetite for validation. Immediately bored and dissatisfied, Miss z turned and flounced through the hotel rotating doors, her entourage clamouring to fall into place behind her.

Miss z made a show of trying to hide her identity as she passed through the dimly lit lobby. A gloved hand shielded her profile as she lowered oversized sunglasses to cover her eyes. Contrarily, she shouted orders to various members of her entourage who frantically made notes, phone calls and frivolous arrangements. She lifted her head slightly and peered over the top of her sunglasses to check that people were noticing her before dismissing the entire entourage at the private elevator, insisting wearily that she was in need of privacy.

Breezing past the two security guards that were posted outside of her suite, she pushed open heavy wooden doors as a wave of cool, clean and expensively scented air enveloped her. Immediately kicking off impossibly high heels, she walked barefoot on warm wood to the kitchen area. She took in the New York skyline through a panoramic wall of glass lining the entire length of the penthouse. There was a time when the incredible view would have impressed her, when she would have stopped to take it in and feel lucky to be where she was. To be who she was. But she couldn't remember the last time that she had felt that way. She couldn't remember the last time that she had really felt anything at all.

Eager for distraction, Miss z let down her hair and pulled off her gloves. She filled a kettle with Perrier and flicked on the switch. Long, manicured nails drummed on black granite counter tops while she waited impatiently. Without anything else to occupy it, her mind deferred to habitual rumination. She fretted over the disappointing performance of her new album. She worried that without fame, money and celebrity, she didn't know who she was anymore. She agonised over the dark insidious mistress that was social media. Everything was terrifyingly precarious.

As she studied her distorted reflection in the cracked-mirror wall tiles, she became aware of the gentle hissing, ticking and clicking noises emanating from the kettle. The sound was warm, comforting and familiar. Her gaze rested on the kettle, eyes relaxing as a strange sense of calm descended. Something profound shifted inside of her and she quietly accepted a darkness that she couldn't quite identify.

Miss z then noticed the wispy steam dancing seductively from the spout, as if preceding the appearance of a Genie. The water began to simmer as the steam came thicker and faster, its dance more urgent. It called to her, and she was inextricably drawn to it. Lifting her hand, she placed it high above the steam. Warm, damp air condensated on her palm. She lowered it closer to the steam, the heat intensifying. It hurt a little, but it also felt good. Curious now, she lowered it further, and further again. The water became excitable as it started to boil. She moved her hand even closer to the rising steam, using her free hand to hold it in place. The pain was intensifying now, but so was the perverse pleasure. It had been so long since she had felt anything like this, since she had felt anything 'real' at all. Miss z was completely in the moment and for once, completely in control. Suddenly she let out a surprised yelp, as her hand flew upwards and away in a self preserving reflex action. The spell was broken as she came to her senses, awoken from her trance. She stared at the kettle, stunned at what had just happened as the switch innocently clicked off. The steam subsided, the dark Genie from within sated.

Miss z looked down at her hand, the skin on her palm angry and starting to blister. The searing pain continued to build as she rushed forward to fill a bucket with ice before plunging her hand into it. The relief was instant, and almost as delicious as the pain that had preceded it. Almost, but not quite…

16 While The Kettle Boiled - High Voltage!

Gary ripped off his high-vis vest and hard hat, throwing both towards the chair in the corner of the portacabin office and missing. Pacing in anxious circles, he shook his head in dismay. Wiping perspiration from his brow with his bare forearm, he pinched the t-shirt away from his sticky torso in order to cool down.

Gary's heart was racing, his thoughts reeling. Agitated and anxious, he didn't know what to do with himself. He just knew that he had needed to get away from the others, to get away from Ryan. But now he was alone with his thoughts, and that wasn't good either. He instinctively reached for the kettle. It was thirty-two degrees outside and as he held it under the tap, he already knew that he didn't want a brew. But he went through the calming motions anyway. He searched in the cupboard for his 'World's Best Dad' mug, a gift from his daughter. He fished around in the drawer for the least dirty teaspoon and tried three cartons of milk from the fridge before finding one that wasn't empty. Gary was lost in forbidden thoughts as he absentmindedly heaped spoon after spoon of sugar into his mug. The gentle tick of the warming kettle brought him back into the present as he realised that his hands were trembling. He set the sugar down and gripped the countertop as if to steady himself, his knuckles turning white with effort.

'What the fuck is going on?' he shouted to an empty room, as he pressed his palms into his forehead. It was too much for him to comprehend, to even allow himself to think about. *Had he just kissed Ryan?*

They had been working together all week installing cables in a tiny electrical plant room; it was a two-man job, but there was barely enough room for one. Initially there had been awkward silences and uncomfortable apologies as Gary would shuffle past Ryan and bump asses, or as Ryan would put an arm around Gary's waist to thread a hard-to-reach cable. But during the course of the week, they had become more comfortable with this close proximity, making less effort to avoid physical contact, and not apologising for it when they did.

On what would be the hottest day of the year so far, Gary & Ryan sweltered. Perspiring profusely, they both swore and cursed. Ryan removed his shirt, making a show of wringing out actual sweat before laughing and throwing it at Gary. His scent filled the small space, a mixture of deodorant, fresh sweat and natural musk. There was nowhere for Gary to put his eyes, he couldn't help looking at Ryan's strong arms as they worked the heavy cables into their housing.

Gary distracted himself with his work, keeping his hands, and eyes, occupied. Ryan reached up to an electrical control panel mounted high on the wall, securing some connections. There was no room to use a ladder and he was struggling to reach. Gary was at least half a foot taller and so he offered to help. He took the power tool from him, feeling the residual warmth from Ryan's hand on the handle. He reached over Ryan's head but it was a little higher than he could reach comfortably and so he extended himself, his t-shirt riding up and exposing bare flesh. Ryan stood with his face just inches away from Gary's chest as he screwed into the wall above his head. Ryan looked down at Gary's exposed stomach and resisted the urge to stroke the swirl of hair that circled the naval before tracing an enticing path into his boxers. As Gary grunted with effort, Ryan looked up at the underside of his tattooed arms, towering above him. A bead of sweat collected in the cute dimple on Gary's chin before falling directly between Ryan's parted lips. Gary stepped back a couple of inches having completed the work. He looked down at Ryan, his chest heaving with laboured breath. Ryan moved forward slightly, closing the gap between them. He lowered his head and gently licked the sweat that had collected in the dip below Gary's Adam's apple.

Gary had a sudden impulse to push Ryan angrily away. To ask him what the fuck he thought he was doing. It was what his brain told him to do, how he had been conditioned to react. But there was another part of him that until now had remained hidden, and that part of him felt very differently. A dormant desire took over his body as he lifted Ryan's chin gently, closing his eyes and the remaining space between them as he kissed him on the lips.

The kettle clicked off and Gary was brought back into the present once again. There was a churning in his stomach, a fluttering in his chest. His breathing was rapid and shallow, and he realised to his dismay that he was aroused. He visibly jumped when a knock at the door filled the quiet office. He instinctively used his hands to cover his erection, but he let them fall gently to his side as the door slowly opened, and Ryan walked in.

17 While The Kettle Boiled - Alison Walker

Alison Walker paused before turning the key, readying herself. She pushed open the front door of flat 5, Cedar Court and stepped inside. As she bent down to gather up the small pile of unopened post she felt a gentle rush of air, as if the flat had been holding its breath.

She made her way up the narrow hallway, trying not to look at the faded framed photographs that lined its walls. Entering the kitchen, she set down the letters and her handbag on the ancient and familiar Formica table. A large clock ticked on the wall as the fridge thrummed in the corner. It seemed surreal to Alison that the clock continued to mark the time, that the fridge continued to cool its contents. She opened the fridge door. Some spoiled milk, a loaf of Nimble bread, an open can of corned beef and a strawberry yoghurt. She had accepted that her grandmother was gone, that she had passed, but until now she had processed her grief only in abstract, as a concept. Dealing with the practical details of her life was different. It brought her back into the present, making Alison feel like she was losing her all over again. It was almost too painful. She gently closed the fridge door. Tea, she thought to herself, she would need tea in order to get through this. Her grandmother had often said that while tea rarely made anything better, it did at least provide one with a distraction in times of difficulty.

Alison disconnected the worryingly frayed cord from the antique Russell Hobbs automatic kettle and swilled it out with fresh water before refilling it. Reconnecting the chunky black plug to the back of the kettle, the kitchen lights dimmed perceptibly as she pressed the red switch to begin boiling the water. She regarded her grandmother's much loved kettle, expensive in its day, and wondered how many cups of tea it had provided over the years. She rolled her eyes at the memory of one of her grandmother's favourite sayings; something about buying cheap and buying twice. A point well made in this relic of a domestic appliance, Alison mused, as a reticent smile hid in the corners of her mouth.

As the kettle hissed and popped into life, Alison checked each room of the small flat. No one had been here since the neighbour, Estelle, had let herself in with a key after becoming concerned that her friend had missed a lunch date and wasn't answering her phone. Estelle had found Annie on the lounge floor. She'd raised the alarm, but they would discover later that she had passed some hours earlier.

Alison hovered nervously in the hallway, peering around the partially open door into the hush of the dark lounge. A shard of light from a crack in the closed curtains exposed dancing specks of chaotic dust. Alison felt a cool draft on her legs. No, not a draft exactly, it was more like disturbed air. Her spine tingled, the hairs on her neck standing on end and causing her whole body to shudder. Feeling suddenly foolish, Alison marched briskly into the dim room, heading for the windows and pulling open the curtains a little too keenly. Light flooded into the room like a tomb cracked open after a millennium of darkness. Alison was surrounded by a veritable treasure trove of knickknacks, trinkets and general plunder collected during her grandmother's life. They filled every shelf, bookcase and windowsill. How on earth would she sort through all of these things, she thought to herself. Precious to her grandmother and therefore precious to her, but worthless to anyone else. She didn't think that she would be able to throw a single item away, and yet how could she possibly keep it all? It was then that she saw the smashed china cup on the floor next to the high-backed armchair where her grandmother had been found. She recognised it instantly as her grandmother's favourite Royal Doulton china and in spite of the trinkets that filled every available surface in the room, Alison suddenly only cared about this one.

She knelt almost reverently to the floor, noticing the tea stain on the carpet. Thinking how upset her grandmother would have been to have broken a piece of her favourite china, she carefully collected up the pieces and held them in her hands. She had watched her grandmother drink from this cup ever since she was a little girl. She tried to assemble the pieces, connecting fragments of rose and golden swirls. It was then that she felt the sudden movement of air again. But this time it came slowly, repeating in gentle wafts. She looked up and saw a reflection in the mirror that hung over the fireplace. She checked over her shoulder for its source, but there was nothing. Looking back at the mirror she noticed that whatever it was, it was moving. Curious now, she got up from her knees and walked slowly across the room to the fireplace, still cupping the broken pieces of china in her hand before her, like an offering. Closer now, she could make out a feint outline of something on the glass. She cocked her head to one side, moving closer still before suddenly taking a quick step backwards as she let out a gasp. It was wings, a pair of disembodied wings! The silver-grey outline was similar to that left behind when a bird flies into a window. But these wings were moving, and they weren't on the mirror, they were *in* the mirror. Alison's jaw fell slack, her mouth agape. As the wings appeared to flutter in slow motion, she felt the air that they displaced on her face. It was fragrant, and comfortingly familiar. Under any other circumstances she might have been frightened, but she wasn't at all.

Transfixed before the mirror, Alison became aware of a mumbling. She tilted her head towards the mirror, tucking behind her ear loose strands of hair that were bothered by the movement of air. She thought that she could hear words, actual words. She strained to listen, but they were just a murmur, too soft and too fast to be intelligible. But there was something inside of Alison that registered them anyway, some part of her that felt the words that her ears could not hear. Without knowing how or why, she knew that it was her grandmother. She'd made Alison feel safe, comfortable. She'd always made Alison feel as if she knew just what was on her mind without her having to tell her grandmother anything. And she had that same feeling now. The murmurings were cajoling, gently persuasive as Alison felt herself nodding her head gently in agreement to something that she felt but did not hear. And then all at once Alison felt a tugging sensation from somewhere inside. It was uncomfortable without being painful, a feeling that something was being extracted, like a bad tooth. There was a build-up of pressure as whatever it was moved closer to the surface and then Alison actually fell forward a little as something heavy and sad finally gave way and was pulled from her chest.

At that moment, the kettle flicked off in the kitchen, the loud click of the switch like the snap of a magician's fingers at the end of a trick, bringing Alison back into the room. She was stunned for a moment, unsure what to do next. She looked down at the broken pieces of china in her hand, only to find that they were no longer broken. Instead, the cup was repaired, or perhaps unbroken, but it was as if it had never been dropped. Alison almost dropped it again in surprise, but managed to catch it, her heart skipping a beat. She was incredulous at what had just happened, but also strangely at peace. Gently shaking her head in wonder and disbelief, a more confident smile now played in the corners of her mouth as she took the precious cup to the kitchen and made herself some tea.

18 A Christmas Miracle

You may have your own idea of what Christmas is and what it means to you. If it means anything at all. I have a complicated history with it myself. A family separation at a formative age forced me to grow up too quickly; it was hard to believe in Santa, Elves and the North Pole when your parents were preoccupied with how much they hated each other, using the kids as weapons of mass destruction as the family fell apart around our ears.

To be fair, once the divorce was settled and we'd all had some time to lick our wounds, dad did his best to restore our belief in Christmas. With the very little we had as a family, he did the most that he could. And I was desperate to believe, happy to buy into the idea of Christmas again, excitedly laying out a stocking at the foot of my bed having set out mince pies and some sherry by the tree. I would be awake into the early hours of the morning listening for the sleigh bells that would precede a thud on the roof. It was ridiculous really; I was well past the age when any of it was appropriate. But I was trying to find my way back to being a kid, to innocence. I thought that if I tried hard enough, if I wished hard enough, then maybe the last few years could be erased, and I could roll back my brain to an earlier version of itself.

I kept up this charade into my teens, a new baby sister providing cover for my childishness. But eventually, reluctantly, I began to let it go. Each year it became harder to reconcile these immature notions with the clarity and cynicism that comes with adulthood. Today Christmas is a bittersweet time for me, steeped in the nostalgia of just a few golden years when life was settled and good, and I believed in magic.

But then something happened. Something odd. More than odd, something fucking weird. And I still don't know how to explain it. Or what 'it' even is. I can't talk about it with anyone because I know how it would sound. How I would sound. But it has made me feel something, remember something that died a long time ago.

***

I've been sat looking at it all day. Sometimes I pick it up, turn it over and around in my hands, the thin, waxy paper enticing under my fingertips. And then I place it carefully on the coffee table again, staring at it from across the room for minutes at a time, lost in thought, revering it like some magical object that has fallen from the sky. What the actual fuck?!

So, backing up to yesterday; Christmas Eve, Eve. I was killing time online by checking Rightmove for addresses I used to live at, a funny little habit of mine. It was something I often did when I was bored or feeling nostalgic. It was almost always a fruitless search, and so I was surprised and excited to see my childhood home appear on the screen before me. It had changed in some ways in the intervening years since I'd lived there, since we'd lived there as a family. New plastic windows were too white against the yellowing and weathered plastic of the adjacent facias. There was also a small extension adding a front porch and, I would imagine, a downstairs loo. But it was still instantly recognisable as...home. I was at once overcome with an uneasy sense of urgency, a sudden compulsion; I had to see it, I had to be within its familiar walls.

The agent was reluctant initially. Being Christmas, they suggested we arrange a viewing in the new year. But I told a couple of small lies and managed to get a viewing for the next morning, Christmas Eve. And so I stood in the hallway of my childhood home, lost in a daydream of reminiscence while Mrs Durrant enthused about the wonderful years she had spent at 38 Downland Road, the family she had raised there and how she and her husband were now planning to downsize and move closer to the grandkids. I took in the space, the energy, tried to feel for a connection, a spark. I visualised the scene around me rewinding years and years, replacing Mrs Durrant and her oak-effect laminate flooring, her freshly plastered walls with my dad, stepmother and baby sister, a worn shagpile carpet and a dado rail separating two different patterns of wallpaper. I tried to conjure a feeling of nostalgia, of childhood, of something. But I could have been stood in any house. There was nothing to suggest that I had ever lived here. That we had ever lived here. That my family had made a mark here in any way. It was crushingly disappointing.

So lost was I in my thoughts that I'd forgotten about Mrs Durrant. Seeing the look of disappointment on her face at seeing the look of disappointment on mine, I thought I had better come clean. I introduced myself and explained that I had actually once lived in the house with my family, that I had hoped that being here again would help me feel a connection with something I lost a long time ago. I'd hoped that my candidness might be disarming, that she mightn't be too upset at my waisting her time. I checked her face for a reaction, but she didn't look annoyed or upset. She just stared at me blankly.

"Sorry, what did you say your name was?" asked Mrs Durrant

"Uh, Paul" I replied tentatively, worried that maybe she was confirming this in order to make a complaint to the agency.

"And you lived here how long ago?"

"Well, I moved out about twenty years ago and dad died a couple of years after that. It was too difficult for my stepmother to stay here, too many memories, so she sold up and moved away."

Mrs Durrant continued to stare at me blankly, but I could tell she was thinking, trying to work something out. She told me to wait there in the hallway before dashing off upstairs and returning with what looked like a small Christmas present. She explained that just yesterday they had knocked out the old built-in wardrobes to the master bedroom. She paused for a moment, checking my reaction for something before continuing. Wedged behind the units she had found this parcel. This present. Mrs Durrant didn't recognise it and had assumed at first that it had fallen down the back of the wardrobe years before, in the time of the previous owner. But then she noticed that it wasn't dusty, that the paper wasn't tatty or ripped. Instead, it was pristine, as if it were wrapped just yesterday. She seemed excited now as she thrust it toward me, telling me to see for myself.

The wrapping paper was vaguely familiar. It was cheap, thin and waxy, like the stuff you used to get at the Christmas market in a huge roll for a quid. It was red, with old-fashioned depictions of baubles and lanterns. Turning it over in my hands, I saw the label. It read *'To Paul. Merry Christmas. Lots of love, Dad xxx '*. It wasn't so much that it was my name on the label that caused the hair on my neck to stand on end, it was that it was my dad's handwriting. I looked up at Mrs Durrant who was clutching her hands before her expectantly, her face full of anticipation. She asked me if Paul was in fact, me. I started to say something but didn't have the words. I looked down at the present again, felt the paper under my fingertips, and followed the contours of whatever was concealed inside. I didn't understand it at all, but I could not mistake that handwriting. And the paper, I remembered it then. Dad had bought a job lot one year, so much in fact, that he wrapped our presents with it every Christmas and never seemed able to use it all up. But that was thirty-odd years ago. How is this in my hands then, I thought to myself.

    I don't remember much of what I said to Mrs Durrant after that. I must have confirmed that it was indeed me, that this was my dad's handwriting. But I remember just wanting to get out of there, to leave quickly in case she tried to take it back from me. I also remember that she asked me if I intended to open it, and the idea of it had shocked me back into the present for a moment. I didn't think that I would, I told her, I didn't think that I could.

***

And so here I am, sipping slowly on a snowball cocktail as I sit alone in my apartment on Christmas Eve. The tree lights twinkle, their reflection dancing on the glass coffee table. I stare at the present. Where did it come from? What does it mean? Does it mean anything? I find it hard to settle on a rational explanation. Logic would dictate that the present has been behind that wardrobe for years, at least the twenty that dad has been dead. But illogically, it looks like it was wrapped just yesterday. You'd think that I would just rip it open. What else is there to do really, how else will I get any clarity on what's going on unless I open the damn thing and see what's inside. I reason with myself that it is most likely an innocently time-capsuled gift from the past, albeit miraculously preserved; special and wonderful, but not inexplicable or impossible. But there is another part of me that wants it to be a gift from the grave, a portentous, supernatural message from my dad. I *want* there to be a logical explanation, but I *need* for there not to be.

But then at once I know I must open it, else sit here forevermore, immobilised in procrastination. There is a sickness in the pit of my stomach and a fluttering in my chest; I can't decide if it is fear or excitement. In a burst of decisiveness, I lurch forward and pick up the gift, figuratively and literally on the edge of my seat. I hold it in my hands and start to become lost once more, the indecision creeping back in. Snapping myself out of it, I quickly rip away the paper. I'm sad for a brief moment as I see my dad's handwritten label fall to the floor by my feet, but it is forgotten as I am suddenly holding a small, plain wooden box in my hands with black with unfamiliar symbols etched into its surface. Gingerly, I open the lid to reveal scrunchy clouds of bright gold and green tissue paper. I pull them out carefully, partly because I am anxious about what I am going to find, but also because I don't want to lose something that might be hidden in the folds of paper. And then I see it, simultaneously realising that opening the present has asked more questions than it has answered.

I pick it up carefully between my thumb and forefinger, rolling it, feeling the worn smooth gold. Could it be? Can it be? I turn it over and around in my hand, looking for the one thing that will confirm it. The one thing that will remove all doubt. I feel it under my thumb before I see it, the rough little snag in dad's wedding band from the time he lost it while gardening, and subsequently found it again with the lawnmower.

The ring had been lost once more when dad was in hospital. It was removed on admission and after he died, was missing from the personal effects returned to us. I had always intended to wear it when dad was gone, and so I had been devastated. But now, after all these years it is here in my hand. But how? None of it makes sense, none of it should be possible. But as much as I know that I may never get a rational explanation, the fact that I am sat here, with this ring in my hand, is all that I care about. I put it on my finger slowly, reverently, the gold feeling cold and smooth against my warm skin. I hold my hand out before me, admiring it incredulously.

Outside, carol singers trim frosty night air with festive spirits. I feel a warm glow and tears on my cheek as they sing my favourite Christmas song.

"Here comes Santa Claus, here comes Santa Claus, right down Santa Claus Lane

Vixen and Blitzen and all his reindeers pulling on the reins

Bells are ringing, children singing, all is merry and bright

So hang your stockings and say your prayers, 'cause Santa Claus comes tonight"

19 I Love You, I'm Sorry, I Love You

Vanessa was uneasy. Butterflies danced ominously in the pit of her stomach as an anxious stream of thoughts raced through her mind. Her left foot tapped a frantic rhythm as she fidgeted with a length of hair, quickly feeding it through her fingers as if raising a tiny drawbridge. She stared blankly at the TV, not focusing on the contestants sat casually around a tackily decorated dinner table as they took catty, delicious chunks out of one another. Instead, she gazed through it, behind it to the wall and then through that and out into the street, through houses, offices, schools and shops and then out of the city altogether, across fields of corn and wildflowers until she was stood before the horizon, caught between a dark, brooding sky and the deep blue sea.

But however far away she imagined herself to be, she could not escape what lay on the sofa beside her, taking up more space in the world than its physical dimensions made possible. She leaned away from it, as if something ominous and heavy were drawing her into its orbit. Since divorcing Dan, things had been difficult. He had not taken it well. At all. And if she was being objective, she couldn't blame him. She had cheated on him under the most appalling of circumstances. After everything he had done for her, all that he had sacrificed, she had left him for her former palliative care nurse. But her guilt was finite. She could only feel sorry for him and disgusted with herself for so long. His constant pleading, harassment and emotional blackmail had eroded her sympathy, twisting and turning it into contempt and disdain.

And so with equal measures of trepidation and irritation, she snatched at his letter. She felt a hard, round disc through the thin paper of the envelope and at once understood what it was that she was holding in her trembling hands. Shocked, she gasped and quickly dropped it to the floor, the terrible thing that lurked inside making a dull clunk as it hit the wooden floorboards. Clutching her hands together against her chest, she stared down at it, trying to fathom why Dan would do this. Did he hate her that much? Using just thumbs and forefingers, she retrieved it from the floor and gingerly removed the letter from inside. She was careful as she did so, not to touch the black velvet pouch that lie in wait at the bottom of the envelope. Vanessa sat down slowly, took a deep breath, and began to read.

Dearest Vanessa

I thought of phoning you first, before sending you this letter. But we don't seem to talk without arguing these days. That's probably my fault; it's taken me a long time to come to terms with what happened between us. It seemed so unfair to me that after all we went through, after what we did and what we survived, that we ended up losing each other in the process.

But that's not what this letter is about. I'm dying, Vanessa. I'm sorry to be so blunt, but what's the point of skirting around it? We've faced death before. For most couples our age, it's a taboo subject, lurking only in shadows and dark thoughts. Not for us.

It is terrifying, and yet also strangely fascinating just how quickly the cancer has taken hold. I've used the little time I have left to put my affairs in order. It didn't take as long as you might think, to tie up the loose ends of my life. I don't know if I should be grateful for that or depressed by it. But my will is filed with my solicitor, who's also the executor, so there's nothing for you to do. When it happens, as my sole beneficiary, she'll reach out to you.

Before I continue though, I just want to say three important things first; I'm sorry, I love you, I'm sorry. However you feel when you reach the end of this letter, whatever you might then think of me, please remember that.

I don't regret what we did. What I did. It's tempting sometimes to think that I might have done things differently, if I had known what would come next. But I don't think that I would have. I'm glad we blew a tyre on the way to the hospital, that we pulled over at those crossroads. I'm glad that I accepted help from whoever that was, appearing from nowhere as I struggled to change the tyre. I'm glad that I broke down in front of him, vented my pent-up frustration and anger about your cancer and the failing treatment. I really think that he believed he was coercing us, tricking us into his confidence. But I had a moment of complete clarity when I accepted the token from him, as incredulous as his words were, as diabolical as his offer was; I both believed and accepted it immediately, without question or hesitation. It was such a desperate time, I would have done anything, believed anything.

But I thought I had more time, Vanessa. That it would be years, decades even before I would be asked to make good on that deal, before he would take what I promised in exchange for your life. I imagined our lives returning to what they had been, before you got ill. I imaged raising a family, kids and grandchildren even. I imagined us growing old and grey together having enjoyed all those years that we were almost denied. And then on my deathbed, I would reflect on all of it, and I would be ready. But things didn't work out like that for us, did they Vanessa?

I'm not asking you because you left me, and now owe me. I'm asking you because you are the only person I can ask. I'm not ready Vanessa. It's too soon. And you have something that I don't. Time. Time to find someone else to give this terrible thing to, someone more deserving of this fate.

I know how incredulous it sounds, what it is that I am asking you to do. Sometimes I catch myself in my thoughts and realise for a moment how insane this all is. That maybe I could just choose not to believe it and it would all go away like a bad dream. But I know that it won't. I know that it's real, despite all logic and reason. I can feel it Vanessa, I can feel him. He's getting closer each day, and I'm not afraid to admit that I am terrified. Not of dying, but of what waits for me after.

You don't deserve this, me putting you in this impossible position. But know that whatever you decide, whether it's to accept the token and free me from this deal, or to throw the damned thing in to the deep blue sea and be free of both it and of me forever, please know these three things; I love you, I'm sorry, I love you.

Forever yours Vanessa,

Dan x

20 Heterochromia Iridium

Matt Hawker woke to the sound of his mother vacuuming the first-floor landing like a cleaning lady on acid. While smoking her third menthol B&H of the day, she charged up and down the hall scrubbing at the carpet like Lady McBeth trying to remove a bloodstain. It was 5.30 am.

"C'mon you little fucker!" she hissed under her breath as she yanked at the cord which had caught on the corner of the banister. He visualised the fag hanging out the corner of her mouth as she muttered and vacuumed, dropping ash on to freshly cleaned carpet.

Bang! Bang! Bang! went the vacuum head against Matt's bedroom door as she enthusiastically worked at a stubborn pile of cat hair.

"MUM! Its still DARK! What are you doing you CRAZY woman!"

He heard his mother kick the vacuum, and again, and again, trying to hit the power button with her foot.

"Fucker!" she yelled as she hit it a fourth time and the vacuum submitted and started to power down.

The bedroom door inched open and the swirl of energy and colour that was his mother poked her head around the crack in the door, bending the end of her B&H as she did so.

"Fuck!", as she examined it for damage. As she talked, she straightened it out a bit, rummaged in her bra for a lighter and relit, taking a deep draw.

"MORNING SWEETIE! Sorry, did I wake you? I was trying to keep it down and let you sleep in a bit, you know, because of your BIG DAY TODAY!!"

"If that was keeping it down, then....God, it is SO EARLY!"

"I know, but I have to get all the household chores done the very minute I wake up, because after a coffee and a couple of fags, I've come around enough to realise that life is too short for this crap. At this point in the day, I don't know any better." She broke into a manic smile. "Well, you're awake now so get up and I'll make you breakfast. I'm making chilli scrambled eggs with roast potatoes".

She pushed open his door and glided into the room.

"Roast potatoes? For breakfast?"

"They're leftovers from dinner last night. It's a shame to waste them".

Matt pulled a face and Lucinda rolled her eyes, took a draw, shifted her weight on to one hip and exhaled; Matt knew that he was about to be educated.

"Matthew, sweetie, people have all *sorts* of potato-based things for breakfast. Hash browns, rosti, potato cakes, sauté, why not roast? I hate all that 'this food is for *breakfast*, this food is for *dinner*, this food is for *people*, this food is for *dogs* nonsense. It's all a marketing ploy to get us buying the same things packaged into different forms to eat at different times of the day. You wouldn't see a starving kid in Africa complaining about being given the wrong *type* of potato for breakfast! Spuds are spuds!! Come on, get up and come down in about 30 minutes. I just need to finish vacuuming and I'll start *'breakfast'*", she said, making theatrical "air quotations" with her fingers and at the same time tapping fag ash onto the floor.

Matt was a little concerned about his mother's lack of distinction between human food and dog food, but he decided not to dwell on it. As he rubbed his eyes and threw back the covers, she turned on her heels and blew out of his room with more drama than was necessary at 5.35 am.

***

Matt had spent more time than he'd like to admit the night before (and the night before that) rifling through his wardrobe to put together his 'first day at a new job' outfit. He didn't consider himself particularly vain but in situations such as this, the right outfit was imperative for him to feel confident. He pulled on his skinny black trousers (were they that tight when he tried them on last night?), his crisp, white shirt and tied his blood-red tie. Slipping on his highly polished patent leather shoes, Matt stood and faced the scrutiny of his full-length mirror.

He did a few lunges and stretches, such as he might be required to do around the office while maybe reaching for a high shelf, stretching to open a drawer at his desk, or bending to pick up the pile of important documents he had just dropped all over the floor. It was snug, maybe even tight, but it looked good, and Matt considered that style would have to triumph over substance today; he could be comfortable later.

He then spent a stressful ten minutes doing battle with his hair, which had picked a fine time to stage a revolution. With not sufficient time for open dialogue, negotiation and other strategies generally applied to such an uprising, he didn't hesitate. Extra product was applied and applied …..and applied until his thick black hair finally yielded into the perfectly manicured, just-got-out-of-bed-look. Surely no-one ever actually got out of bed with hair like this, Matt thought; the look was painstaking to achieve.

A few more ablutions, mirror checks and hair adjustments later, Matt decided he was good to go, and headed down for breakfast. As he entered the kitchen, he was greeted by his mum shimmying to Lady Ga Ga playing on the old and tinny but ridiculously loud, vintage transistor radio. If Lady G were dead, he thought, she would be turning in her glittery, egg-shaped grave.

Lucinda popped and convulsed her body wildly as if in some kind of electric shock induced seizure.

"Ooh, there ain't no other way, baby I was born this way, BABY I WAS BORN THIS WAY!!" as she

marched around the kitchen singing into an eggy spatula.

"I LOVE this song, Matt. Who sings it?" she managed to get out between the chorus and the next verse.

"Lady Ga Ga, mum – though you wouldn't know it from *your* rendition".

"Don't make fun of your mother. And Baby *who*?"

"LADY, not *BABY*"

"*LADY* Bah Bah? Never heard of them!"

He laughed, despite himself. He sat down at the kitchen table as Lucinda scooped onto his plate steaming piles of fluffy scrambled egg, flecked with shocks of red chilli.

"Mum, this is amazing! Honestly, it's delicious" he said with a mouthful off egg and potato, some of it flying across the kitchen like a small yellow missile, landing neatly in the cat's food bowl.

"Why thank you Matty, I'll forgive your earlier rudeness".

Matt ate his breakfast, drank his coffee and checked his phone. While he waited for Facebook to refresh, he looked around the kitchen as if seeing it for the first time, the way you do sometimes when your mind stops racing ahead to the next thing for a moment. He enjoyed the heady aroma of cooked eggs and freshly brewed coffee, and the ever present warm, hazy smell that was emitted by the ancient (and probably dangerous) gas hob. He traced the knots of wood on the old kitchen table with his finger, felt where he had carved his initials when he was a kid, the deep indentations once fresh, sharp and bright against the dark wood, but now worn smooth and diminished over time.

The kitchen was Lucinda's favourite room in the house and was where she spent most of her spare time. If she wasn't cooking, she would read, sat in an old, battered armchair in the corner of the kitchen by the back door, or rather than use the front room and watch the 50" plasma TV that Matt had bought last Christmas, she would sit in the same armchair and peer into the old portable TV sitting on the breakfast bar that sometimes, depending on atmospheric conditions, got colour.

It was in this very kitchen, one wet and cold Sunday afternoon that Matt had come out to his mother while they prepared a meal. Considering how open and organic she had been about almost everything in his life, he had been inexplicably anxious about telling her. It was not that he expected a bad reaction; he knew she would accept it. It was more that he hadn't said it out loud to anyone before. He was worried about how he'd feel once it was out in the open. It was one thing to be notionally gay, to live out fantasies in his head and to dream. But once he started to tell people, it would become a reality. He would have to stop hiding.

He had been busy frying onions while his mother grated carrots when he had clumsily blurted it out. Initially, Matt thought she hadn't heard him as she didn't respond straight away. Her grating of the carrots simply slowed, until it stopped altogether, grater and half a carrot held aloft, motionless. It took Lucinda just a moment to regain her composure; she had been waiting for this revelation and knew that her response would matter to Matthew; she wanted so much to get it right.

"That's nice dear, but be careful you don't burn those onions", as she leant across him to turn down the gas on his ring.

He had stared at her for a moment, blinking, not sure what had just happened. Had she heard correctly? Had she absentmindedly answered a different question, one that she thought she had heard? Squeezing out excess juice from the carrots into a glass bowl, his mother could feel his eyes on her, waiting. She'd turned her head to look at him, giving him a little wink and a crooked smile as she bumped his hip with hers.

"Matthew darling, being gay is just who you choose to love. So, you love men? That's just wonderful - I love them too! But it doesn't have to be a lifestyle; it doesn't have to define you as a person. It just means you are attracted to men. Everything else is up to you. Keep an open mind Matty and try new things, experiment. It's an exciting world out there!"

Matt couldn't believe that he had just come out to her, and *she* was telling *him* to keep an open mind. It obviously hadn't come as a surprise to her, he'd thought. Her words were carefully chosen, having the quality of something she had agonised over, rehearsed and now repeated at the appropriate time. And they were exactly the words that he had needed to hear, even if he hadn't known what they were until his mother had spoken them.

***

Matt shouted farewells over his shoulder as he pulled the front door shut behind him. Feeling the sharp November air on his face, he instinctively shrugged up his shoulders and wrapped a scarf around his neck. He took in a deep breath as he swung open the squeaky front gate, leaving the safety of home and stepping out into the big, wide world. Matt walked carefully on the icy pavement, starting to regret his choice of fabulous, but completely grip-free shoes. He had butterflies, his stomach a flutter with both nerves and excitement. He'd applied for the position of junior office administrator at a large insurance company having come to the realisation that his job at the men's clothes store wasn't going anywhere. He'd made some good friends there, some he even hoped to stay in contact with after leaving. And he'd enjoyed working with the general public. Most of the time. But it was a dead-end job and although Matt didn't consider himself the career type, he did understand that in order to live the life he wanted, he was going to need a better job.

As he turned the corner and approached the bus stop, the camber of the pavement conspired with a patch of ice to send him flying forward into a man standing at the back of the queue. Instinctively, Matt put out his arms as he fell forward and grabbed hold of the innocent, unsuspecting stranger. He hit the ground with a thud, a rip and a 'fuck'. His face turned crimson and burned with embarrassment as he felt himself lifted to his feet by two strong hands. He looked up into the most mesmerising, beautiful pair of eyes he had ever seen. One glacial blue, steely and penetrating and the other the colour of amber, warm and inviting.

"Blimey, are you alright?"

"Ugh, yeah, I'm fine. I think" Matt said, breaking the stare of those impossible eyes. "I'm so sorry, and so embarrassed. I….I'm…. well….." Matt stammered for something to say that might convey his apology but at the same time claw back some dignity. He bought time by brushing off dirt from his coat and straightening himself out. When he looked up again, he took in the man's full frame. He was a good 5 inches taller than himself, slim but with wide shoulders, strong jawline, swept back blond hair and….those eyes. He flashed Matt a smile, which was akin to being struck by lightning. There was a glint in his eye and a quirk to his lopsided smile that conveyed bemusement rather than any kind of aggression, or annoyance. He wore a tailored navy suite, a dazzling white shirt and a sky-blue tie, over which a grey felt overcoat clung to his body, emphasising his height and broadness.

"I'm sorry. It's the ice and these damned shoes. And I think I ripped something", he said as he twisted round to look at the back of his trousers.

"I think you're fine, that ripping sounds was my pocket tearing off as you tried to tackle me to the ground". He held it up for him to see and for reasons Matt will never understand, he gently took the torn piece of felt from him, holding it carefully in his hand, as if it were something sacred.

"Oh crap, I'm so sorry. Let me get it fixed or buy you another one or something. God, I'm so embarrassed".

"Don't be embarrassed, it was an accident. To be honest, the coat was a present from my girlfriend, but I always thought it made me look a bit of a twat. So maybe you did me a favour" he said, flashing him another playful smile as he stroked his lightly stubbled chin. Matthew was put at ease by his light heartedness and laughed a little, albeit awkwardly.

The stranger put out his hand.

"I'm Tristan by the way".

"Hi, I'm Matt".

Matt looked up at Tristan as he shook his hand, their eyes locking as everything around them became suddenly, very still.

A strange sensation washed over Matt, he was at once flushed, in spite of the biting November air. An unstoppable wave of excitement surged through his body as he felt Tristan's hand in his, their skin touching, electricity crackling. Tristan tightened his grip, gently squeezing Matt's hand. It was intimate, strong and reassuring. Tristan then pulled Matthew gently toward him, their eyes still locked on one another, and Matt had the undeniable feeling that something incredible and life changing was about to happen.

Tristan was overwhelmed, a tempest of conflicting emotions raging inside of him. Excitement, desire and infatuation battled with fear, anxiety and confusion as he tried to make sense of what was happening. He was rooted to the the spot, unable to move, unable to release his grip of Matt's hand, unable to break his gaze, and yet there was also something inside that was telling him to run, because following this path would lead to him deep into the unknown where he would be exposed, and vulnerable.

In just the few seconds that passed, a deep understand of something fundamental had been relayed between them. Something that couldn't be measured or quantified, something that once felt, would change everything, forever.

With a hiss of brakes, the queue came suddenly to life as commuters, shoppers and school kids jostled to alight the bus, breaking the spell that had briefly bound them together. Tristan quickly broke eye contact with Matt, embarrassed now, and suddenly ashamed, he pulled his hand away from Matt's and shoved it deep inside his remaining pocket. He looked around himself nervously to see if anyone had been watching.

"Well mate, look after yourself and, um, well, watch that ice!" he chimed brightly, and louder than was necessary. Matt remained thunderstruck, and after an awkward pause, Tristan turned and leapt onto the bus, leaving Matt alone. With his hand still outstretched, Matt's mouth opened and closed, the power of speech deserting him.

As the bus pulled away, Tristan tried desperately to forget what had just happened. He pushed it deep into that crowded room at the back of his mind where he hid the terrifying feelings that he sometimes had for other men. But he couldn't help himself. He turned in his seat to look back at Matt and saw him stood where he had left him, motionless and limp, head down, shoulders drooped and arms hanging sadly by his side as if he was slowly deflating. He was still holding Tristan's torn pocket in his hand. It was both the saddest and sweetest thing that he had ever seen. And there it was again! That connection, a jolt of electricity and a surge of energy that forced him up and out of his seat and towards the front of the bus. He didn't know what he was doing, or what he was about to do next, but as he yelled at the driver to stop and let him off, he had complete and utter clarity of the fact that he wasn't able to do anything else.